Edwin DeLeon

Under the Stars and Under the Crescent

Vol. 2

Edwin DeLeon

Under the Stars and Under the Crescent
Vol. 2

ISBN/EAN: 9783337348724

Printed in Europe, USA, Canada, Australia, Japan

Cover: Foto ©Andreas Hilbeck / pixelio.de

More available books at **www.hansebooks.com**

UNDER THE STARS

AND

UNDER THE CRESCENT

A ROMANCE OF EAST AND WEST

BY

EDWIN DE LEON

AUTHOR OF "KHEDIVES' EGYPT," "ASCABOS CASSIS," ETC.

IN TWO VOLUMES

VOL. II.

LONDON

SAMPSON LOW, MARSTON, SEARLE, & RIVINGTON

St. Dunstan's House

FETTER LANE, FLEET STREET, E.C.

1887

[All rights reserved]

CONTENTS.

CHAPTER XVIII.

CHAPTER XIX.

CHAPTER XX.

CHAPTER XXI.

CHAPTER XXII.

CHAPTER XXIII.

CHAPTER XXIV.

CHAPTER XXV.

UNDER THE STARS AND UNDER THE CRESCENT.

CHAPTER XII.

THE SULTAN'S SELAMLIK.

An animated and excited group was assembled in the salon of the Grand Hotel, after an early breakfast of the most substantial kind, which the French *chef-de-cuisine* had prepared for the American party. For it was Friday the Mussulman Sabbath, the day on which the Sultan is alone visible to the unbeliever and to the outer world, going and returning from the midday prayer, chiefly at the mosque of Beckishtach near the palace of Dolma Bagtche, his chief residence.

The inevitable dragoman or guide-
interpreter was present, of course ; and so
was the cawass or guard of the Legation,
the old Mohammed Aga, who after twenty
years of service could speak about a dozen
words intelligibly in the Anglo-American
tongue : but whose portly form arrayed in
gorgeous uniform, and dignified deport-
ment, inspired respect among the vulgar
for the parties he escorted, even from the
small street boys, more demonstratively
fanatical than their elders.

The dragoman, on this occasion, was an
old man of Greek origin, who had had a
most adventurous career, and who spoke
pieces of most languages more or less
imperfectly. A fine hale hearty ruddy-
faced old man, Yanco or John by name.
He had served famous men in confidential
characters, and proved himself worthy of   ·
their confidence. From General Williams,

the hero of Kars, and from the equally famous Hungarian General Klapka, he bore the highest testimonials. With the calmness and collectedness of superior knowledge and long habitude, he imparted fragments of information in broken English or French to the eager girls, as to the sights they were about to see, and the personal peculiarities of the ruling Sultan, the central figure of the weekly pageant. Many of the details perhaps would not have undergone strict examination, for even the Sultan himself is not above and beyond the inexhaustible gossip and fertile invention of the population of Pera, to whom might justly be applied the remark made by " the Prophet " in his haste, "that all men were liars," together with the Scottish divine's commentary, that had the Prophet chosen, he might have repeated it at his leisure.

From the Grand Hotel in the Rue de Pera to Bechishtach, wherein is the mosque chiefly visited by the present Sultan, is a distance of about two miles : which you can traverse in a carriage over very tolerable roads, passing very numerous and very grand-looking barracks, in which are quartered the many thousands of troops with whom the Sultan loves to surround his person and palace.

Descending in front of a guard-house painted bright yellow, our travellers, through the kindness of their Armenian friend, were allowed to enter a small building facing the mosque, in which were congregated the aide-de-camps, marshals, and other high dignitaries of the empire, who were not expected to accompany the Sultan from his palace, as were his more immediate *entourage*, but who, on his arrival, sallied out and joined the cavalcade.

Every Friday witnesses the same procession, the same ceremonies, and the same proceedings. At midday precisely the Sultan leaves his palace, either in a carriage or on horseback. He is preceded and accompanied by a large number of troops of the line and cavalry, both presenting a martial and imposing appearance, for the garrison at Stamboul is well-fed clothed and cared for, whatever may happen to the civil employees, the population at large, or soldiers in the provinces. Nobody knows accurately how many thousands this garrison numbers, but it is very large.

On they came with loud blasts of trumpets and drums, and clash of warlike music. There is a Sultan's march, of course, composed by obsequious Europeans and dedicated to his Imperial Majesty, who is said to be a great lover of music.

After the troops have filed past, or formed a living lane through which the Padischah is to pass, securely fenced in from his loving subjects, who swarm like bees—a few Christian wasps among them —over the pathway : a *cortège* of state carriages, conveying the high functionaries of the empire, military and civil, heralds the coming of the Sultan in person. A splendid Persian carpet is immediately unrolled from the door of the mosque down the steps, to the spot outside where the foot of majesty might otherwise come in contact with the earth on which common mortals tread : and every particle of dust is persistently brushed from the carpet by obsequious slaves, until the imperial foot rests upon it. The high functionaries, marshals, chamberlains, ministers, and the officials of the royal household, range themselves on each side of the steps, awaiting the arrival of the august one. Sometimes he comes in a carriage, but if the weather be propitious rides up on a white Arab charger, as proud and pampered as the master he bears.

This was what they saw. The Padis-chah of all the sovereigns of the earth, *Imam Muslemin* (Chief of the Faith), Zil-Ullah (Shadow of God), Hunkiar (Man-Slayer), and bearer of other high titles, was a stout powerfully-built man, with a broad jovial face, and rather dissipated look.

On his face there was not the shadow which is supposed to cloud the counte-nance of those doomed to sudden and tragical deaths, such as that which befell him, the mystery of which probably never will be fully cleared up, although Midhat and other high functionaries underwent trial, conviction, and punishment as ac-cessories to his murder.

It was but a glimpse of him which the spectators caught, as he descended from his horse, assisted by obsequious atten-dants, and passed up the steps into the building.

The uniforms of his marshals and suite, as well as those of his ministers and high functionaries, were stiff with gold em-broidery, and covered with glittering decorations from the Sultan and from foreign potentates. It seemed strange to see the cross of Christian monarchs decorating the breasts of these scoffers at that holy emblem ; and equally strange that they should wear it even in the presence of the head of their faith. If the disem-bodied spirits of the fierce founders of Islam, or those of their equally fanatical adversaries, the Crusaders, can revisit the scenes of their former conflicts, astonish-ment must blend with wrath at such a

sight : if the passions of this world survive
in the next.

Contrasted with these gorgeously-attired
officials, the severe simplicity of the
Sultan's dress attracted the attention of
the foreign visitors. He was attired in
the Stambouli or Frank dress, with its
straight coat-collar, like that of a clergyman of the Church of England, without
decorations, a diamond aigrette in his red
fez being the only ornament, and more
conspicuous through that simplicity than
his glittering retinue. What surprised
our American friends not a little, was to
observe that not only men stood awaiting
the Sultan's arrival, but that a line of
women, closely veiled, occupied the front
rank, just outside the line of soldiers which
hemmed in the sacred person from any
outside intrusion. The mystery was explained as the Sultan rode up. For then,

when a shrill but feeble cry of welcome rose up from the ranks as the Sultan passed (so unlike the cheer which would have echoed there from European throats), every woman's hand held up and fluttered in the air, what at first seemed like a white handkerchief, but was in fact a petition addressed to the Commander of the Faithful in person, and which by ancient usage he is supposed to receive and determine upon, without the intervention of his ministers.

Whatever the fact may be, officers of the Sultan's household certainly came, and carefully collected all these petitions, both from men and women, and all went away content, in a confidence which perhaps may have been justified. It was thus that King Solomon sat in judgment at the gate, and the *Sublime Porte* is the shadow of that ancient ceremony, as its name imports.

In the meantime the two young Americans were not left to the mere contemplation of the glittering parade passing under their eyes ; but became the centres of much attention, from the younger portion of the Court *attachés* congregated in the small building, which served as their observatory. Among these were their friend the Armenian aide-de-camp, and several of his brother-officers, whom he introduced to them; and keeping shyly in the background, they also recognized the striking face and figure of the young hero of the steamboat accident, Selim Pacha. But he, with true Turkish stolidity, neither by look nor gesture indicated any previous knowledge of them, which called forth from Lillie Hancock, the petulant remark,—

" I suppose that young man must have heard the story in England of the gentleman, who could not save a drowning man

because he had never been introduced to
him. He really is too good-looking to be
so stupid as not to be presented to us, when
he must know we are dying to talk to him."

"Speak for yourself, Lillie," laughed
Helen, "I do not care if I never set eyes
on the young man again, nor how many
Turkish young women he may fish up out
of the Bosphorus. I am not such a man-
eater as you are."

"No," answered Lillie, petulantly, "your
taste has become more juvenile, since that
smooth-faced Armenian boy, who seems
half girl, has filled your fancy. For my
part I prefer a man! and the Turk looks
one, every inch of him."

An angry flush passed over the fair face
of Helen at her friend's sharp speech, cutting both ways, and on the tenderest spot;
but feeling herself no match for that quick-
witted damsel in the war of words, she bit

her lip and was discreetly silent. But
although Selim Pacha did not approach and
ask an introduction, many others did, attracted by the bright fresh faces of the two
American girls. The foreign officers in the
Sultan's service, French English and German, together with a few Armenian civil employees, buzzed around them like gilded flies.
French was the universal language spoken,
and the girls improved the shining hour
by making themselves agreeable to the
miscellaneous crowd of admirers. The
reckless and lively Lillie attracted the men
more than her far prettier but more gentle
and timid companion.

Old Celia was with her young mistress,
and her astonishment at the confusion of
colours in the faces of the Sultan's suite
was extreme. But her indignation was
roused, and her anger beyond bounds,
when she saw and was informed of the

special functions and privileges of the black Kislar Aga, or head-eunuch, and witnessed the profound respect with which he was treated by the highest functionaries of the empire.

" Well," she sniffed, " tings is turned topsy-turvy in dis here country, and no mistake. It used to be mighty mean bizness to be oberseer on South Callina plantation ; but dis obersein of wimmin in the Sultan's big house, and a spyin' arter 'em, and a drownin' 'em if he catches 'em at tricks, is a ting dat de meanest plantation nigger down Souf couldn't be hired to do."

Neither did the veiled ladies of the Sultan's harem, whose carriages preceded his, escape her severe and caustic criticism.

" Call dem wimmin good-lookin', Miss Helen, wid dere great big saucer eyes, painted black underneat, and no sense in 'em, staring tro' pieces of gauze at ebbery body?

"Calls em modist, does you? Why nebber in all my born days did I see such a set of brazen-faced lookin' huzzies. No wonder de men has to shet 'em up and put guards on 'em. Why down Souf, you kin see more rale pretty galls. in one hour, dan you kin find here in a week. An den, bout dem wails. I notices one ting', wen de woman young, and tink herselb pretty, she wear mighty tin wail, jist like cobweb; but she werry partiklar to hab tick one when she ole and ugly. But I suppose wimmin all same 'bout dat, Miss Helen, all ober de worle."

Helen recognized her admirer, Pancaldi Bey, in a handsome uniform, which set forth his slight boyish figure and hand-some face to great advantage, in attend-ance on the person of the Sultan, his duties not permitting him to join the group in the guard-house. All this was going on while the Sultan was dismounting from his charger, and up to this moment he had ridden like a blind man, through the lane of soldiers, fenced in by the outer crowd of spectators, making no acknowledgment of his reception, but staring straight on vacancy.

But on ascending the steps of the mosque, and reaching the door, he turned around, and facing the multitude, made a slight and almost imperceptible gesture, in shadowy imitation of a Papal benediction : and followed by his functionaries disappeared within the mosque, to repeat his *Namaz* or morning prayer, which comprises the Moslem Pater and Credo, and which by law and usage he must thus publicly repeat on each successive Friday, by law and custom of Islam.

His failure to do this, unless prevented by serious illness, would be bitterly resented by the fanatical Ulemas or priests, who constitute the most dangerous political class at Constantinople : as the Sheik-ul-Islam, or head priest, can issue a *fetwa*, or Pope's Bull, declaring the Sultan to have violated the law of Islam and his duty, which would be a warrant for his removal from the throne, by force or otherwise. This and assassination are the only two checks on this absolute ruler.

An hour spent in the mosque, partly in prayer, partly in giving receptions to a favoured few, in a room assigned him there for that purpose—and the weekly ceremony was over.

But during that hour the *cortège* remained, and the opportunities of conference among the high officials, and of intrigue, were largely profited by. The

assemblage of so many notables gave full
scope for such manœuvres, and many a
fortune was made or marred, many a job
pushed onward to completion during that
hour. Then the Sultan issued forth again,
attended by the same pomp and ceremony,
and returned to his palace, to be invisible
for another week. Among those honoured
by imperial recognition on this occasion,
was General Prescott, whose card, according to usage, had been sent to the
Sultan after prayers at the Selamlik. An
aide-de-camp came and tendered him the
the Sultan's felicitations on his arrival for
the purpose of entering the service, with
some flattering expressions of imperial
pleasure, in having secured so distinguished
a soldier. The promise was also given of
an early audience, the time of which would
be indicated to him.

CHAPTER XIII.

THE CEREMONY OF THE HIRKAI CHERIFF.

A WEEK later another opportunity of seeing the Sultan in public presented itself.

It was the season of the Ramazan, the great Mohamedan Lent, when for a whole lunar month, from sunrise to sunset each day, no morsel of food, no drop of drink, and no whiff of tobacco, is permitted to soil the lips of the conscientious Mussulman.

Even the higher pachas, who privately may violate the Prophet's injunction, seldom dare to do so in public; although a dispensation for ill-health, travelling or time of war, may be granted by the ulemas.

Evidently borrowed from the Christian Lent, Ramazan has its *Mi-Carême* or Mid-Lent as well. For on the fifteenth day of the fast, the great ceremony of the Hirkai Cheriff, or veneration of the Prophet's Mantle, one of the most solemn and imposing of Moslem religious ceremonies, takes place with great pomp and public demonstrations, presided over by the Sultan himself. As this ceremonial chanced to fall on Friday, a double duty had to be done.

The Sultan and his court first attended religious services, at the famous historical mosque of Aya Sofia, once the Christian church of Santa Sophia, and then proceeded to the ancient palace of Top Kapou, founded on the site of the summer palace of the Byzantine emperors, amidst the once

lovely but now neglected gardens of the
Seraglio Point, still a glorious shadow of
what once must have been a terrestrial
Paradise. In that palace are deposited
two of the most sacred relics of Islam, the
Prophet's Mantle of camel hair, concealed
by fifty coverings, embroidered with verses
from the Koran,—and the Sacred Banner,
never brought forth save on some great
crisis of the State.

The one awakens the pious veneration
of the faithful, as connected with the
person of the Prophet; a relic as precious
in their eyes as a portion of the "True
Cross" to the devout Catholic. The other
awakens the fierce fanatical instincts,
which under its folds swept the Mussulman like a devouring flame over Asia and
Europe. The last use to which this dread
banner was put practically was, when
Sultan Mahmoud II. displayed it to the

populace and soldiery, just sixty years
ago, when he determined to destroy the
Janissaries revolting against him.   On
that occasion it was proven that the old
spell still lingered in its folds, and his
appeal was successful, with what result
we know.   Thenceforth it has rested
quietly under its gorgeous coverings, only
to be reproduced at a moment of similar
peril to Sultan or empire.

The *Hirkai Cheriff*, is the camel's hair
cloak of the Prophet.   It lies in a
sanctuary, enveloped in fifty coverings,
richly embroidered with verses taken from
the Koran.   No eye but that of the Sultan
may look on the uncovered relic.   He only
may remove all the coverings.   For the
rest of the faithful two only of the outer
coverings are removed by the officiating
ulema, or priest, and the hem of these
they may kiss, entering by one door and

retiring by another, so as never to turn
their backs on the sacred relic. No
Christian may witness this ceremony,
which is reserved for the true believer
alone. But all the world may witness the
outdoor ceremonies, and the pomp parade
and military display which accompany
the Sultan in his passage from his 'palace
to Bechishtach, through Tophane, Pera,
Galata and Stamboul, to the mosque of
Aya Sofia, and the old palace on
Seraglio Point—a spectacle of rare splendour and striking originality.

At one o'clock the Sultan left his
palace in an open *calèche*, accompanied by
two of his grand marshals inside, and a
cavalcade of cavalry outside; passing
through streets, which were but a lane of
soldiery, for the whole distance of three
miles. Thousands of spectators thronged
the houses, the house-tops, and the streets,

through which the procession passed.
Up to the private entrance of Santa
Sophia, specially reserved for the Sultan,
these guards surrounded the sovereign.
The court carriages, hundreds in number,
of which eighty were occupied by the
inmates (male and female) of the Imperial
palace alone, followed the Sultan's carriage.
In the mosque he said his *Namaz,* or
prayer, according to the ritual ; and this
ended the first part of the day's ceremonial.
An hour later he issued forth from the
mosque, and in a grand state carriage
drove up to the *Bab Hommayon,* or gate,
leading up to the palace of Top Kapou or
Seraglio Point.

The Seraglio Point—the most attractive
spot to the historian, as to the traveller
whose eye rests on its verdant enclosures
with delight each time he passes up and
down the Bosphorus, or skims in his

caique over the Golden Horn—is the central point of Constantinople. From the hour when the conquering Mohammed II. pitched his tent there, and built a royal residence, it was the head-quarters of the Ottoman dynasty.

For a thousand years it had been the imperial residence of the Byzantine emperors, whom he displaced. For fifteen centuries it had been the cradle of Imperialism—Christian and Moslem—until Abd-ul-Medjid removed the royal residence to the palace of Dolma Bagtche, which he caused to be built on the opposite bank of the Bosphorus.

Twenty-five Sultans resided here from the commencement down to the decadence of the Ottoman power in Europe. Foreign ambassadors who displeased the Sultan were imprisoned in one of the seven towers, down to the days when the

English ambassador, Lord Stratford de Redcliffe, was the actual as well as titular Sultan.

Built on the eastern hill of Stamboul, on the European shore, overlooking the Sea of Marmora, the Golden Horn and the Bosphorus—with Asia frowning across the narrow strait from Scutari, where the true Moslem alone will be interred (as the true Mussulman resting-place, for their living as for their dead, when Europe shall reclaim her own long-lost territory),—the collection of palaces on this hill constitute a Grand Memorial.

Up this verdant slope to the old place of residence of the Byzantine emperors, to the rejoicing shouts of *Padischahim tchok yasha* (Long live the Sultan), came their successor, to worship the real or supposed relic of the Prophet of Islam, enshrined on the spot of former Christian habitation.

The crumbling and broken walls which surround the former stronghold of Stamboul, as of Byzantium, attest the decadence into which both have fallen in the lapse of those centuries; and from the heights afar off tower the mountains of Bithynia, in Asia Minor, crowned by the snow-capped Mount Olympus, overlooking Broussa, first seat of the Ottoman empire.

Type of change and of modern progress, a railway now passes under the crumbling walls of the seven towers, where ambassadors were imprisoned of old.

In the palmy days of the Ottoman empire, foreign ambassadors were received at the palace on the hill, "between two walls of silk and gold," according to the ancient chronicles; and thousands of attendants, dressed in picturesque liveries, attended on the court circle, numbering many thousands more. Now the suc-

cessor of these kings of the world passed
up the hill into solitude and silence,
through deserted gardens and palaces
falling into decay and ruin, with only a
few kiosks now habitable. The " Gate of
Felicity," which formerly led to the harem
of the Sultans, is now virtually closed : for
the cage no longer contains the birds as of
yore !

There he was met by the *Cheik ul Islam*,
high priest of Islamism, the shadow of
the head of the Faith (the Sultan), who is
Grand Caliph ; and by the Grand Vizier and
other high personages, who followed him
into the sanctuary wherein the sacred relics
were deposited. He made his devotions to
these relics, and then the others followed,
himself retiring into the apartments of the
old palace.

Here he remained, until the gun at
sunset announced that the faithful might

break their fast; when he partook of the *Iftar* or evening meal, and returned across the Bosphorus, with the same pomp and state, to his palace on the opposite side.

Conversing with an intelligent French resident at the hotel after his return, General Prescott commented on the fervour of Mussulman belief in the Prophet, and the fanaticism, which his relics and the sacred standard still inspired in the Turkish mind.

This led to some conversation on the subject, which induced the Frenchman to ask if any of the party had read a recently published book, by Vicomte Alfred de Caston, which gave two curious illustrations of Moslem toleration and respect for other faiths than their own. On being answered in the negative, the Frenchman went to his room, and produced the book, from which he read two extracts bearing on the subject.

The Vicomte de Caston thus describes a conversation between the famous Fuad Pacha and himself :—

"One fine morning in the month of August, I accompanied his Excellency Fuad Pacha, then just recovering from an attack of the cruel malady of which he subsequently died, on a sail down the Bosphorus, to visit Aali Pacha, then Grand Vizier.

"As we rowed down near Bebek, with our three pair of oars, in the caique, the wind was so strong that we stopped a little. In front of us was an immense building, only partly constructed and still unfinished. The sun shone splendidly, and the unfinished structure let in the light on all sides, as neither doors nor windows obstructed it. Through the

openings the sun streamed in everywhere.

" ' How many windows, do you think,
are there ? ' inquired Fuad Pacha.

" ' I cannot say accurately—perhaps a
hundred,' was my reply.

" ' A hundred windows,' said the pacha.
" Yet the same sun shines into each !
It is the same with the different religions,
which should unite, and not divide the
human race. There is but one God, for
the heaven and for the earth, and the
love of this all-powerful Master penetrates
our hearts through a hundred different
Mezebs (churches).' "

" Very liberal, and very philosophical,"
said General Prescott. " Now for the
reverse of the picture ! Only yesterday,
while making antechamber at the Sublime
Porte, awaiting an appointment with the
Grand Vizier—but never kept by him—I

met, in the crowd of expectants, a young
Turkish officer fresh from Paris. In the
course of conversation he propounded to
me a puzzle, which has perplexed wiser
men than myself.

" Pointing to the motley crowd which
surrounded us, he said,—

" ' We have in this room an orthodox
Greek pope (or priest), an orthodox
Armenian, a Roman Armenian, a Maro-
nite christian, a Papist and a Protestant
christian—all claiming to be Christian
priests.

" ' Now, monsieur, I understand that
you Americans have many other varieties
of priests outside of these. Give me your
advice. If I wished to turn Christian, to
which of these should I give the pre-
ference ? '

" As I hesitated how to answer the question, he said laughingly,—

" ' On the whole, I think I had better wait until they agree among themselves ! ' "

" Oh, yes," replied the Frenchman, " that young officer was doubtless one of the new school, partially educated abroad, who have become as cynical and sceptical in all matters of faith, as any Parisian *flaneur*, lounging over the asphalte of the boulevards. But the better class of the old-school Turks, as well as of the new, unspoiled by foreign contact, have pre- served intact their sense of reverence, and (as their fathers did) respect not only the name of Mohammed but that of Jesus (Issa, they call him), in only a lesser degree.

" The Arab founders of the Moslem faith, who were an imaginative race, have many legends which embody the popular belief. In those legends the names of Issa, and of Mariam, his mother, are always reverentially treated, as are also those of Moses, Abraham, and the prophets. Here is one relating to the birth of Jesus, recorded in this book. Let me read it to you ! "

This was the legend which the French author had reproduced in all its native simplicity, which ran as follows :—

The Legend of Issa.

" Allah, pitying the misery of mankind living in darkness and ignorance, resolved to send them a great Prophet, and chose one of his well-beloved angels to spread the divine light among benighted mortals. This angel was charged to make a tour over the earth, and search from what household should be born the Infant, which should live the life of man, and suffer all its pains, for the glory of Allah ! After one moon the angel returned, and reported : 'After traversing the universe,

and visiting all its great capitals and
palaces, I finished by finding one just
man, in the little village of Nazareth.
This was an honest tradesman, named
Youssouf (Joseph), who lives in the fear of
Allah, and is always helpful to his brother-
man.' The angel added, that this man's
wife, Mariam, was the wisest and most
virtuous of all women.

" Allah was well pleased with the
manner in which the angel had performed
his mission; and immediately gave orders
to the angel Gabriel what to do.

" The night had come. Youssouf had
gone to do some work in a neighbouring
village. Mariam reposed alone. The
archangel Gabriel descended from heaven,
and without awakening her, laid beside
her on the couch a lovely rose, plucked in
Paradise ! The next morning at dawn,
Mariam awakened, and beheld the Infant

Issa, who smiling, stretched out his arms towards her."

" How charming! and how poetic ! " cried out Helen. " I had no idea that there was so much imagination in the Mohame-dan legends ! This one surely is worthy of being embalmed in verse by some Eastern poet ! Has it ever been ? "

" I do not know," answered the French-man, " but its spirit breathes that charity to all men which is the essential principle of Christianity ! "

" I shall never have any patience with people after this, who talk about Moslem intolerance," said the girl warmly—and her friends, in their hearts, echoed the same sentiment.

When Helen, later in the evening, repeated the legend to her Armenian admirer, and enthusiastically praised

Moslem tolerance, he shrugged his shoulders, and with something very like a sneer writhing his thin lips, responded,—

"Yes! the Turks are quite as great makers of fine phrases as the French, and are as much in earnest. The very soul of their faith is narrow intolerance, as their history proves, and my race and family have good cause to know what their tender mercies are. The deadliest enemies of the Turk are within his own household. The Rayahs (native Christians), all sigh for the hour, while watching and waiting its coming, when they shall be freed from his heavy yoke, and Constantinople again become a Christian capital.

"If, as the Scripture tells us, 'a house divided against itself cannot stand,' surely the Turkish empire in Europe must be tottering to its fall."

CHAPTER XIV.

THE table-d'hote at the Grand Hotel was both a study, and a source of infinite interest and amusement to the newly-arrived Americans. The Grand Hotel deserved its name, for it was an imposing building, with a fine entrance up a lofty flight of marble steps, a dome above, and plants in graceful vases filling the niches beside the stairway.

Ascending the marble steps you reached a fine large hall with lofty ceiling, the walls of which were adorned with almost priceless tiles, framed in squares or oblongs,

and with the Eastern pictures of the
local artist Prezioso, certainly the most
accurate and correct of any delineations of
those subjects by any artist of far greater
renown. Connoisseurs know how to prize
these pictures, but the fame of the artist
(now dead) has never been commensurate
to his merits, or to the work he lived to
accomplish.

Passing through a door on the right, you
enter the dining-room, a large, airy, and
very handsome one, capable of containing
a very large number of guests.

Around the long table-d'hôte, which ran
through the centre of the apartment,
twice each day were congregated guests of
the hotel, numbering usually from thirty
to forty persons, and often double that
number, comprising specimens of such
varied nationalities, and giving such a
feast of languages as well as of food, as

it would be hard to find out of Constantinople.

Here sitting amicably side by side and
interchanging opinions and news, might be
found daily representatives of almost all
nationalities, two alone among which did
not cordially assimilate, the French and
the German, neither of whom have yet had
time to forget Sedan. There was a small
sprinkling of ladies, but the great majority
were men, attracted to or detained at
Constantinople by business or by the hope
of business, in the shape of railway or
other concessions, which the Turkish
Government, while professing willingness
to grant, almost always contrived to avoid
giving.

Of the permanent residents who congregated at the upper end of the long
table, every man had a history, and an experience of the country and its adminis-

tration, for which he had daily paid in time, trouble and hard cash, and generally speaking had reaped only that experience for his expenditure.

There were men sitting at that table who had sat there for years, in daily expectation of finishing affairs of importance with the Turkish Government, the completion of which had been solemnly promised them shortly after their arrival, with the utmost fervency and apparent sincerity by the Sultan's ministers. There were others who had been waiting and still were waiting to receive payment for goods and materials furnished the Government, who like the unhappy Theseus in Virgil's Eneid sat and eternally would sit, waiting in vain for what never came.

The patriarch of these waiters on Providence and the Turkish Government, was an Englishman, a man distinguished

throughout life for his energy and successful enterprise, for which he had received
the recognition of his sovereign in the
shape of a title, the last man one would
have imagined it would be possible to
play such a game with, as that which had
baffled him for eight long years, during
which time he had never left the country,
nor seen his family. He told the sympa-
thizing American girls that he had left a
little girl of two years at home at his
departure, who now, at ten years of age,
would certainly not recognize him on his
return. He explained to them the endless
procrastination, and equally endless
cunning devices of the Turkish officials,
which had delayed and prevented the
settlement of his just claims, and the
ingenuity of those processes was only to
be surpassed by their utter unscrupulous-
ness. He opened their eyes to a system

of bribery (here termed backshish) pervading every department of the state from
the head, through the members, and down
to the lowest extremities of each administration, and the utter impossibility of
reaching the only fountain of authority,
the Sultan : around whom a more than
Chinese wall of exclusion was built up and
jealously guarded. There was but one
possible way of reaching his eye and ear,
and that a dubious one, and that was on
Friday, when he proceeded to the mosque
to say his prayers, to stand on the route
of his progress, and attempt to attract
his notice, by waving in the air a petition
setting forth the subject of complaint.

This system the old gentleman declared
he intended to adopt on the ensuing
Friday, almost farcical as seemed such a
sequel to his long eight years of effort and
argument, to obtain an act of simple

justice, and the restitution of his own fraudulently withheld from him.

It is a pregnant commentary on the mode of doing business in Turkey, and of the proper mode of trying to do it, that this apparently absurd and desperate resort did finally succeed: and that the indomitable Englishman, by this method, did obtain a final settlement, by which he recovered a small portion of what was due him, by making a compromise; and shaking the dust off his weary feet went home, with the fixed intention of having nothing more to do with the Turkish Government.

Next the Englishman sat a French naval officer, whose trials had only been of months not of years, but who chafed and fretted under them with the constitutional excitability of his nation. He had come, by special invitation of the Government, to

conclude a contract with the Minister of
Marine (Hassan Pacha) for a certain
number of steamers—the terms of which
contract were fixed in advance—subject
only to the successful trial of one, which
was to be tested in the presence of the
Turkish officials. He had successfully
performed his portion of the agreement,
the Government had taken possession of
the boat he had brought, and expressed
perfect satisfaction with it: and the
Minister of Marine had forthwith proceeded to attempt an imitation of it in
the arsenal workshops, and for eight
months, under frivolous pretexts, had frus-
trated the formal ratification of the contract the Government was in honour bound
to make, after the successful trial. Wearied
out and disgusted by such treatment,
and foreseeing no practical conclusion
to a business thus conducted, the French

company had indignantly ordered the return of their representative, and lost all hope of either persuading or compelling the Minister of Marine to act in good faith.

The indignation of the French naval officer found vent in open denunciation at the table.

" On my return to Paris," he said, " I will get the meanest cur I can pick up in the streets, shall put a brass collar round his neck with the name of Hassan Pacha and fez on his head, and kick him around my room every morning to give me an appetite for breakfast."

There were men of almost all nationalities sitting at the table, similarly situated to those two mentioned, with more or less of hope of concluding the business which had brought them there, all of whom confirmed the correctness of the

statements made : yet each of whom in his
secret heart cherished the hope of arriving
at a more satisfactory conclusion, through
some influence purchased from the subordinate officials, or high officials near the
Sultan himself, or through superior management of their affairs.

All agreed that could the Sultan personally be made to know of the proceedings
of his officials, their tenure would be short,
and· business be done on quite another
basis ; but all equally coincided in the impossibility of reaching him, except by the
merest accident or blind chance.

Not alone Europeans congregated at that
table, but Greeks, Armenians, and educated Turks as well, all with a job or a
grievance clinging like a shirt of Nessus
to them, and bearing unmistakable traces
in their worn faces of the incessant grind
and worry to which they had been and

were still subjected. Some of these were
Government employees or officials, whose
pay was only semi-occasional, and who
therefore had perforce to live on pilfering
from individuals, that which the Government did not give them for their mainte-
nance. Others had been suddenly turned
out of their posts by secret intrigue,
without any specification of charges or
opportunity of defence, and were seek-
ing restitution. Added to these were
the tourists, not of the "personally
conducted" Cook class, who did not
patronize the Grand Hotel, but foreign
princes princesses counts and countesses
by the score, eminent politicians, poets
and artists, and travelling Americans all
"sovereigns" by virtue of the Declaration
of Independence, and stray diplomats, who
had "left their country for their country's
good," as Barrington said of the convicts

at New South Wales. The confusion of tongues was rendered greater by the diversities of language. French Italian English Greek German Roumanian, Armenian and Turkish all being used, and flowing in separate rivulets constituted the sea of conversation. For the study of languages by ear no better position can possibly be found than a seat at a table-d'hote at Constantinople; although the stranger gets terribly bewildered at the confusion of the sounds which fly around him. Probably nowhere—save in the United States—can such a profusion and variety of fish flesh fowl game fruit and vegetables be found, as at one of these table-d'hôtes, and the delicacies of Turkish cookery and Turkish sweets blend with the European in their cuisine. The gourmet has nothing to complain of there except surfeit.

Yet the guests, especially the English, will grumble even here, and the latter will draw disparaging contrasts between the roast beef of old England and the flesh of the Eastern kine ; and while revelling in the grapes of midwinter, scornfully contrast them with the hot-house fruits of Albion.

The table-d'hôte at Constantinople is an epitome of the world, and nowhere are extremes brought more closely together than there.

Could some cunning Asmodeus unroof the skulls of the *habitués* at the Grand Hotel of Constantinople, what more than Asmodean mysteries and strange stories would not that process reveal? But happily life consists chiefly of externals, and so long as those present pleasant features to us, it is wiser not to pry and peer into depths which conceal ugly realities, and repulsive memories.

Let us enjoy the *menu* of the table-d'hôte, without searching for the skeletons which may figure at the feast.

CHAPTER XV.

BAKALOUM AND SOCIETY AT CONSTANTINOPLE.

In the days of the Patriarchs, when human
life had its span of nine hundred years,
time was by no means so great an object,
in the settlement of affairs, as in these our
more degenerate days when men live
fast and die fast, and the Scriptural limit
of threescore and ten is exceptionally
reached. One of the cousins of Me-
thusaleh, for example, having business
with that celebrated personage long ago,
might conveniently have postponed it for
fifty years or so, and finally been none the
worse for that comparatively brief delay.
But days now count, as years did then;

yet the conservative East still keeps up the old system of hope deferred, and perpetual procrastination, and "*Bakaloum*" (We shall see about it) is its watchword. As *Bakaloum* means indefinite postponement and polite evasion, the soul of the stranger, awaiting that which never arrives grows sick within him; and his watching and waiting become a weariness to his flesh and to his spirit.

So did it fare with General Prescott and his American colleagues, when day after day and week after week passed wearily by, and they received from the Seraskier or Minister of War, on the rare occasions they could get a glimpse of him, only evasive answers to their urgent pleas for formal admission to the service and active employment. Bland and polite that functionary was, profuse of phrases, and of coffee and cigarettes ; but of performance of his promises no signs were given. He showed a great curiosity about things in America, but carefully avoided reference, or direct reply, on the matters which brought them there. The dead wall of no common language gave him a great advantage in this respect; and the interpreter was entirely too well-bred, to insist on answers his Excellency obviously did not care to give. The old general pulled fiercely at his snowy moustache, after each abortive interview; his impulsive young aides expressed their impatience and disgust in the strongest Anglo-Saxon, when out of his presence, but suppressed their feelings before him; amusing themselves, as best they might, in excursions with the ladies of the party, and the new acquaintances they had made in the society of Constantinople. This society they found to be very curiously constituted and divided, like ancient Gaul according to Cæsar, into three parts.

The first part, which overshadowed all the others—as Mount Olympus does Broussa on the smiling plains of Asia Minor—was the diplomatic corps! with its caudal appendage, in the shape of what considered itself the Society—a curious compound, the title to belong to which could not possibly be defined, since many were in it who ought to have been out of it, and many out of it who had every possible right and claim to be in it.

There was not only one diplomatic court but many, like rings within rings, or nests of pill-boxes at the pharmacies: each ambassador holding his own petty court, and lording it over a coterie of his own nationality. The awe and reverence inspired by these self-created magnates surpassed the comprehension of our

Republican friends, for their followers spoke of them ever with bated breath and whispering humbleness; although those foreign representatives were certainly neither (men or women) above, if equal to the standard of foreign representatives elsewhere. But not to be admitted into this charmed circle was considered to be out of the world in Pera, and on the Bosphorus: and innumerable were the heart-burnings occasioned by invitations to or exclusions from it.

Another branch of Constantinopolitan society, partly in it though not of it, and dwelling much apart from the rest, was to be found in the small colonies (chiefly English) established at Candili, Kadi-Keui on the Bosphorus, as also the Princes' Islands on the Sea of Marmora. These latter were quiet, sensible people: professional and business men, with their families, domestic in their habits, and caring nothing for fashion, but much for health and comfort—by far the most substantial and sensible portion of the foreign population. They mingled but little with the other circle, except on public occasions.

A third division was made up of the Greek, French, and Italian residents, who enjoyed themselves in their own way, and had their own separate entertainments, less pretentious, less stiff, only far more gay and joyous than the more highly starched society of the diplomats and their satellites. But into this latter society the English-speaking population rarely ventured; changing their climate, but not their habits of thought and action.

Of native society at Constantinople there was none. Neither the Turkish men nor the Turkish women encouraged association with the "Stranger within their gates."

At the formal diplomatic reunions of the ambassadors of foreign powers, a few Turkish officials might occasionally be met with; putting in an appearance, as a matter of etiquette, by permission of the Sultan, and the intercourse was limited to such interchange of civilities. But there was no intercourse at all between the Turkish and foreign women, nor were the former disposed to encourage efforts on the part of the latter to break down the harem barriers; although from curiosity they might occasionally allow strangers to visit them.

The American girls, and their young countrymen, soon found the Perote society very wearisome; local gossip constituting the chief theme of conversation, and scandal its cream. If this

composite population, made up from
Europe and the Levant, were as " wise as
serpents " in all worldly matters, it certainly was not as " harmless as doves " in
social converse; since even personalities
were not considered piquant, unless
compromising character, and concealing
venom.

" Malice hatred and all uncharitable-
ness " seemed to have pitched their tents
with the Christian colony on the Bosphorus,
and permanently abided with and amidst it.

In that society there figured some
remarkable men whose lives had been passed
in the Turkish service ; notably a pacha, of
Italian origin, who since his childhood
had filled public positions, and now, at an
age when most public men seek the well-
earned retirement their life's work entitled
them to, was still actively engaged in a
high diplomatic post. His career had

been one unbroken series of successes.
He had represented Turkey in Italy and in
Russia. He had been, for ten years,
Governor-General of the Lebanon, and was
promoted thence to another high mission.
He was a small, wiry, active man, with
prominent features, and eyes which still
brightened at the view of a pretty woman,
or of a political antagonist. An old
school courtier, of the highly polished
school of former times—bland, persuasive,
ever polite, but concealing " the hand of
iron under the glove of velvet," he had
kept peace between the Druses and the
Maronites of the Lebanon, as no governor
ever had before. Speaking almost all the
languages of Europe, his conversation was
full of interesting souvenirs, though he
was no egotist ; being too much of a man of
the world to fall into that fatal habit. Yet,
during his forty years of public service in

East and West, he had picked up many
curious incidents, and could narrate
strange things. Especially of his experiences in the Lebanon, that debatable land
of Christian and Turk, and of Druse—who
can justly be classed neither with the one
nor the other—the most mysterious of all
the Eastern races. There was also a
secretary of legation, of French origin,
whose life had also been passed in Turkish
diplomacy; and who, commencing his
career under the auspices of the pacha
just mentioned, still continued his *rôle* in
connection with his old chief, though
gradually rising in position. He was a
young man comparatively, probably forty
years of age, a remarkable linguist both
as to Eastern and European languages, a
strikingly prepossessing person both in
face and figure, and yet, with a modesty
which contrasted strongly with the brazen

self-assertion and conceit of the *attachés*
of the foreign embassies, to whom he
could have taught the rudiments of their
common profession, and the chief outlines
both of literature and history.

It certainly tells well for the Turks, that
they have had the sagacity to appreciate
and secure the life-long services of two
such foreigners, as the pacha and his
secretary of legation: neither of whom
ever swerved a hair's breadth from his
principles or his religious faith, to conci-
liate any of the fanatical prejudices which
might have barred his advancement in the
public service, but openly professed and
practised the observances of the Catholic
faith, which was their inheritance. In
Turkey, as in Egypt, there were many
Europeans, who for the sake of advancement, apostatized and adopted the creed
of Islam. But these men never secured

the confidence and respect of the Turk as
thoroughly as those who, while faithfully
serving the Sultan's Government, disdained
to do so.

A third conspicuous foreigner, whose
death cast a gloom over the whole Perote
society, and even extorted the tribute of
sincere regret from his rivals in the Turkish service, was a Turco-English admiral,
whose life and adventures constituted a
romance in this prosaic century of ours.
Younger son of an English nobleman, at
an early age he entered the navy, and was
known as a gallant and dashing officer in
that service, when the war broke out in
the United States between the Federals
and Confederates. His imagination was
fired, and his excitable spirit kindled, by
the risks and chances of blockade-breaking.
He obtained a leave of some duration,
and, under an assumed name, was one of

the most daring and successful of the blockade-breakers.

His *naive* recital of his adventures while playing this *rôle*—just previous to his entering the Turkish service—amused and interested the girls beyond description ; and in him General Prescott found a genuine sympathizer and friend, in this remote and alien land. Although a leading member of society, he was in the habit of laughing freely at and criticizing severely its affectations and absurdities. The lash of his fearless tongue scourged many of the popinjays attached to the embassies, as well as the pretensions of those high and mighty persons themselves, who handled him as cautiously, as discreet persons would an explosive bomb-shell.

There was a foreign society also, composed of Levantine families, that is of persons of foreign descent for several generations, born and bred in the Levant, and this was a far livelier and more amusing collection of people than the diplomatic circle.

There was far less of pretension, and far more of enjoyment in their *réunions ;* but the English-speaking part of the community had nothing to do with their festivities.

So there were many divisions and sub-divisions in the small European colony of Pera ; and many were the bickerings and heart-burnings engendered by the fierce strife for position and social recognition among them.

The happy few who, from their official position, could walk or drive out, accom-panied by a gorgeously arrayed *cawass* or guard, inspired the envy of those less favoured by governmental selection ; and such attendance gave a brevet rank, and

was a substitute for a decoration. Some
of those not entitled to the cawass
ex officio, attempted a substitute, which
passed muster to the eyes of the unini-
tiated, by getting a *Croat* attendant, whose
dress as closely resembled that of the
regular article, as *vin ordinaire* can be
made to supply the place of *Chateau
Margaux.*

One of the most agreeable and cultivated men they found among the diplomats was the Persian ambassador, whose
European training at Paris and elsewhere
had made him more than half a Frenchman ; while his domestic life was Eastern
on one side of his house, European on the
other!

His dinners were worthy of the *Champs
Elysées.* His conversation of the full
French flavour. His appearance, when he
kept on his high conical Persian cap, tho-

roughly Persian; when he took it off, thoroughly European.

He was the living embodiment of two separate and widely different nationalities rolled into one. His mental characteristics were also as varied. One of the astutest of diplomats in a country where diplomacy is a science, he was also a poet and an historian. He had also successfully played the *rôle* of a soldier in earlier days, and thus first won the favour of his sovereign, having encountered the invading English force at Bushire, in the year 1857; and for two years he remained in the army. He then went into diplomacy, and at Paris London Berlin and Belgium, showed high capacity. At Constantinople he was equally popular with Turk and with Christian, and his portly figure was seen conspicuously at all the diplomatic *fêtes*, into which he entered with the zest and freshness of a boy. His wife—a cousin of the Schah—lives in Eastern seclusion, on the harem system.

A Persian ambassador, who has translated Fenelon's "Telemachus" into his own language, and who can make himself understood in English as well, can boast of being a polyglot, without undue assumption of vanity. Such a man is Mohsin Khan. There are few men who can live two lives as he has done—that of the East and that of the West—and this Oriental continues to do so. Which he prefers it is impossible to ascertain, probably difficult for himself to define.

These were among the few bright spots to be found in the higher heavens of the diplomatic society; and its larger and lesser stars revolved monotonously and drearily in their own restricted circle,

during the winter at Pera, during
the summer at Therapia and Buyukdere
on the upper Bosphorus; following a
routine of receptions, dinners, and garden-
parties, each one more wearisome than the
other.

The Anglo-French daily press of Pera
chronicles all the proceedings of *High
Society* with unfailing punctuality and
minuteness, and equally unfailing notes of
admiration.

Every ambassadress "received her
guests with her accustomed grace, and
urbanity," on every occasion. Every
entertainment was "gay and brilliant,"
and a happy few even had their costumes
chronicled as well; and what more could
the heart of woman desire ! Among these
editors were some clever men, but they
were as Pegasus harnessed to a water-
cart ! so restrictive were the Press laws,

so stern the censorship of the Ottoman
Government, seconded and often pushed
on by the diplomatic body, which allowed
no freedom of comment on theirs or their
Governments' acts or intentions. As a
caustic writer observes : " One could write
and publish freely what one chose, *provided* it was nothing that could displease
the Ottoman Government or its ministers,
the foreign representatives, the heads of
the numerous religious communities, nor
the directors of public institutions or
companies, nor any one connected with
the palace or public administrations, or
persons in any way connected or influential with the Empire."

But General Prescott did receive an
invitation to a military dinner, given by a
General of division to his soldiers, on the
occasion of a great religious festival, which
kept up the traditions of Eastern polite-

ness, and was most poetic in its style. It
ran as follows :—

In the name of Allah !

" HONOURED SIR,

It is my humble request, that
you will be pleased, graciously and con-
descendingly to honour with your presence
the Lamb Feast, to be given on the 26th
(Friday) to the ever victorious Imperial
troops ; who are as the apples of our eyes.
It is our purest desire, and we venture to
request that you should attend ; and thus
plunge us, unworthy, in the sea of happiness !

" (Signed) HASSAN PACHA,

" *Muchir* Commanding troops."

Of course, to an invitation thus worded
refusal was impossible—and the Lamb
Feast was honoured by the American
General's attendance, that the native
guests " might be plunged in the sea of

happiness," from whence they emerged with amazing appetites—devouring such quantities of lamb, as revived the memories of Gargantua, the father of the great Pantagruel, as chronicled by Rabelais.

The two girls had been to their first ball at Constantinople, which had been given at one of the embassies, where the cream of society, and some of the skimmed milk also had been collected. People supposed to be somebodies, and people considered to be nobodies,—but in that transition stage, which divides the chrysalis or the grub from the butterfly,—had been congregated together, had simpered smiled at, elbowed and envied each other, and, like the two devils in Gil Blas, had "embraced, and secretly sworn eternal hatred," as is the wont in all countries.

The impressions produced on the two

girls were widely different. Helen, in
the full flush of youth simplicity and
enthusiasm, had enjoyed herself, because
she had had partners for every dance, had
utterly demolished her satin slippers, and
received the devoted attention of her
Armenian admirer,—who, arrayed in a
becoming uniform and decorations, was
quite a man of mark, and an intrepid
dancer. Lillie on the contrary who had
sprained her ankle, and was therefore, contrary to her wont, compelled to sit down
all the evening among the non-dancing-
guests, could not enter into the whirl; but
had to play the part of an observer only.
Luckily however, she found in the lady who
sat near her most of the evening a good
Samaritan, from whose witty and racy
conversation she derived both amusement
and instruction, regarding the chief
characters figuring on the social stage

before them. After her presentation to the ambassadress, who received her with frigid courtesy, and took no further concern about her, Lillie subsided into a convenient arm-chair, and surveyed the motley group of all nationalities, and in all possible or impossible costumes, that buzzed and swarmed, like a hive of bees, through the Grand Saloon appropriated to the reception.

The American girl was much amused at witnessing the marked difference in the manner of the hostess towards her guests, as they successively presented themselves ; exhibiting freezing civility and lofty condescension to some, a slight thawing towards others, and a perfectly melting mood and easy familiarity towards the favoured few.

The lady who sat next to Lillie, to whom she had been introduced, was an old

resident—an Englishwoman—Mrs. Downright, whose intellectual brilliancy and
fearless independence had survived even a
long course of Perote and ambassadorial
entertainments, where flunkeyism and
toadyism and abject reverence for position and wealth are the rule, not the
exception. The bright black eyes and
sarcastic tongue of Mrs. Downright were a
terror and a corrective to the inane men
and women, who formed the majority of
that society, and her friendship was as firm
as her enmity.

She took a fancy to the frank fearless
young American girl, and took the trouble
of enlightening her as to the things and
personages which attracted her curiosity.

Turning to her neighbour, Lillie said,
" The ambassadress seems to have a good
many different manners for her guests.
I have remarked her reception of them

seems to differ most materially, and to be
registered by almost every different degree
of the thermometer ? Why is this ? Pray
enlighten my Republican ignorance, for I
am sure you understand the reason ? "

" Certainly," answered Mrs. Downright.
" She has one manner for her associates of
the charmed circle, the diplomatic corps ;
another for the favoured few unofficial
people admitted into it, and a third for the
great majority of common mortals outside
of it : permitted like Moore's Peri, to
linger at the gates of Paradise only, but
not enter it."

" Why ! " said Lillie in astonishment,
" are the diplomatic circle of Constantinople supposed to be made out of better
clay than the rest of mankind ? or are they
so infinitely superior in birth culture
intelligence and manners to the rest of
the society, that it is considered honour

enough to let them breathe the diplomatic atmosphere, with the privilege of being snubbed by those semi-royal personages? Or are we admitted on sufferance to their 'palaces,' as they call the embassies here, though nowhere else in the world?"

Mrs. Downright laughed. "Yes, my dear Miss Hancock, such is exactly the case! No matter how well born well bred cultivated or intelligent you may be, you are a nobody at Pera unless you are connected with the diplomatic circle!"

"What rubbish!" said Lillie indignantly.

"Of course it is; but the toadies here encourage this high mightiness on the part of the diplomatic corps, and fawn upon it. So the consequence is the members of the sacred circle get a most exaggerated idea

of their importance, although most of them
were nobodies at home, and soon sink to
their proper level when transferred to
other foreign posts. There was one
little creature here who is greatly re-
sponsible for all this nonsense—almost
a gorilla in appearance—with morals
as bad as his manners, who, having been
transferred to an European capital, has
found his proper level there, and writes
most despairing laments for his lost glories.
Voltaire asks, what can be thought of
a people who have an ape for their god?
We had one here, but are happily rid of
him ; but the evil he did lives after him."

" Ah," said Lillie, " I see a thaw in
our hostess' frozen manner, somebody is
arriving ! Who is that short stout vulgar-
looking woman, full of fuss and finery, who
is just arriving ? "

" My dear, you are irreverent ! That is

the ambassadress of a great power, one of
the divinities. She was reputed to be a
very 'fast woman' once, not only with
one, but with many histories ; but she is
slow enough now, and has a habit of falling
asleep at her own receptions."

"But she still has admirers," said
Lillie, "look how those supercilious-looking
young fellows, who have been lounging
about the door-ways, regardless of the
really pretty girls I see around us, have
suddenly awakened, and crowd around
her ! "

"My dear ! she is one of the sacred
circle. What more is required ? I really
begin to fear I cannot sufficiently impress
your Republican simplicity with the awful
import of that word."

" I hope not," said Lillie. "I have
seen a good deal of nonsense going on in
foreign courts—according to my Repub-

lican ideas—and have laughed at their
absurdities; but anything equal to the
pretensions put up by these pigmies in
diplomacy I never did see, and would not
care to see much more of. It is perfectly
nauseating, and I cannot see how high-
spirited and intellectual people like you,
who must despise it as much as I
do, can put up with such insolent conduct."

Mrs Downright smiled satirically; but
her bright eyes beamed approval of Lillie's
honest indignation.

"My dear young lady," she said,
"when I was your age I was as full of
contempt for the follies and the false pretensions of my neighbours as you are,
but I have long since abandoned the battle;
and accept the situation. Here one must
either swim with the current or be
drowned. So I keep quiet, and like the

rest of mankind, submit to be patronized by our 'little tin gods on wheels,' as your Boston satirists term such people."

"But," asked Lillie, "is there no other society here except this pasteboard imitation of a court circle?"

"Yes; there are several societies, composed of different nationalities, which have a lively time among themselves. The foreigners, as we call everybody not English, the French Italians and Greeks, keep up their own festivities in their own circle, and very jolly they are. I mix a little with them, and find their parties very pleasant, even without the fine flavour of the diplomatic essence. Do not laugh too much at English toadyism, for it runs in the blood, and some of the most servile specimens of flunkeyism out here might be picked out among your own American people residing here. Some of these are just as badly bitten by this social tarantula as any of our own people, and crawl after their highnesses, the ambassadors, on all fours."

" As I am going away soon," answered Lillie, "it does not matter for myself. But I hope my dear little friend Helen will not be inoculated with this dreadful malady. I am quite sure the dear old General, who is a born Republican aristocrat, and considers himself the equal of any prince or diplomat, will tolerate no such nonsense."

At last Helen, having danced herself into a state of exhaustion, was ready to leave, as Lillie and the General had been hours before; and the ambassadorial entertainment dissolved itself, as such empty pageants do, leaving a few pleasant and many unpleasant recollections in the minds of the crowd assembled at the semi-imperial invitation.

" Well," said Lillie, as she and her
friend disrobed and jumped into bed, just
as the dawn began to peep into the
windows of the Grand Hotel, "if this
be a fair specimen of the balls here, I must
say that one of them is a full dose ; and
I shall not care to repeat it. Everything
there seemed to be well frozen, including
the hostess, and it resembled more a mas-
querade than a private party. Everybody
seemed acting a part. A more utterly
artificial display I never witnessed ; and the
patronizing airs of our entertainers were
simply insufferable to anybody with the
least self-respect."

Helen, weary but happy, yawned and
replied,—

" Oh, Lillie, I found it lovely ! I danced
every time," and so their colloquy ended.

Such were the chief features of society
at Constantinople at its two extremes.

CHAPTER XVI.

A CONFERENCE AND A PLOT.

As Lillie Hancock sat alone in the salon, at the *Grand Hotel*, on the morning succeeding the Sultan's Selamlik—the rest of the party having gone on an excursion which she did not care to join in—a waiter entered, with a visiting-card, on which was inscribed the name of Selim Pacha, aide-de-camp to his Majesty the Sultan.

She had been yawning over a French novel of the new realistic school, which even its impropriety could not render interesting, the pervading flavour being that of sewerage, but this unexpected visit roused her immediately out of her languor, into a flutter of expectant curiosity.

" What can the man mean by calling on me specially," she thought, " and not even asking for General Prescott, my father, or Helen ! They tell me he spent some time in Europe, and is acquainted with the usages of society there. Well I shall soon find out."

" Ask the gentleman to walk up," she said, and the waiter retired.

A few moments later he returned, ushering in the young pacha, who stood before her after making a respectful bow, with embarrassment depicted on his usually impassive countenance, seemingly at a loss how to commence a conversation. Lillie saw his confusion ; and, with her usual readiness, came to his assistance.

" Pray take a seat," she said, " I am most happy to see you, for I recognize in

you the gallant rescuer of the lady of
the caique on the Bosphorus. My father
and friends have frequently expressed
their great desire to make your acquaintance! And you know General Prescott
is soon to be a comrade of yours, in the
Turkish service? They will be so sorry to
have missed you this time, but you must
accept me as their substitute."

The embarrassment passed like a
shadow from the young man's broad open
brow, at this cordial greeting. He drew
a chair near Lillie's, seated himself, and
bending towards her, said in a low voice,
in French, "Lady, mine is not a ceremo-
nious visit! I come on a mission to you
from a lady you know. Emineh Hanum
sends these as my credentials," and he
handed to the now startled girl a card, on
which a few lines had hurriedly been
traced.

There were two sides to the complex
character of Lillie Hancock, and the
earnest and serious traits were immediately
awakened by the few words the card contained; while at the same time wonder
and curiosity were aroused in equal proportions, as to the connection existing
between the writer and the young man
who now sat grave collected and impassive
by her side.

The rapid glance she cast on him, blending these various emotions, he immediately
appreciated with the quick perception of
an Oriental, with whom looks mean more
than speech.

" Lady," he said, " you are naturally
astonished at such a. communication
coming to you and through such a source,
having learned, as you must already, that
our ways are not as your ways, and that
no acquaintance, much less free inter-

course, is permitted between a young man and a young woman here, as in your more fortunate lands of the west. You doubtless suppose Emineh Hanum to be a Turkish girl, but she is a Christian like yourself by parentage and by choice ; and the accident which made her know me you yourself witnessed. It is due to her as well as to yourself, that you should understand how I chance to be her messenger, and what relations exist between her and myself. The whole truth shall be made known to you, and then you can judge whether the hope of deliverance she has placed in you has any foundation. But do not misjudge her, nor me, although I am a Turk in blood, in training and in faith. But I have lived in other lands, and unlearned much, else should I not be here, pleading with a Christian woman, to deliver a sister from the prison of a Turkish harem.''

In brief but explicit terms Selim then related to the highly-excited and deeply-interested girl, the story of his visit to the harem and interview with Emineh ; omitting only the concluding portion relating to his encounter with Mejnour as personal to himself.

Lillie listened to the narrative with absorbed attention ; the romantic side of her nature was deeply stirred, and the confidence reposed in her flattered her self-love, and roused her energies to prove herself worthy of such sudden trust.

" The story you tell me is a strange one," she said, " the confidence reposed in me is stranger still, and the service required may entail danger to others, if not to myself. But everybody says I am a queer girl, and I shall not shrink from making the effort you ask, when I know what I am to do and how I am to manage it. This your experience of the country must suggest."

" Lady," gravely responded Selim, " the task you are to perform, is neither so diffi- cult nor so dangerous as you might readily imagine. Turkish women have more free- dom of action, or at least of movement, than you suppose in your ignorance of their ways; and you can easily rescue Emineh Hanum if you choose."

" How? explain yourself! " answered Lillie briefly, fixing her bright blue eyes full on the face of Selim.

" Simply by asking her mother to allow the young Hanum to take you to the bath of Galata Seraï in Pera, near your hotel, with her next Friday. There are two doors, a front and a back one. She can change her costume there, slip out of the back door in disguise of a European woman, be conveyed on board the ship which sails for France at two o'clock that day, and be far beyond pursuit or capture long before any one dreams of her flight. Once in Europe she can rejoin her father. Suspect you as her mother may, she can prove nothing against you, and you and your friends have nothing to fear from her or from the Turkish Government, which dare not interfere with you, even if a proof could be produced against you."

"A very pretty plot," said Lillie, laughing merrily. "Why it reminds me of Opera Bouffe; only you sit there with such a solemn countenance while proposing it. But it does look easy the way you put it, and I feel half inclined to try it." And the reckless girl laughed again so long and loudly, as utterly to disconcert the dignified Turk, whose knowledge of the ways of foreign women was extremely limited, in despite of his foreign travel. "But tell me," she said, with a sudden return of gravity, "what, in heaven's name, has induced you to trust me in a matter like this, where an indiscretion on my part would so fearfully compromise you, and possibly cost Emineh her life, if half the stories I hear be true. I have the credit at home of a warm heart, but my most partial friends never accused me of discretion."

"Ask that question of Emineh Hanum, not of me," replied the young man. "I am but her messenger. She believes that she can trust you, that is sufficient for me. As for myself," he added, drawing himself up proudly, "the hand of Selim Pacha has never yet failed to guard his head in the hour of emergency, nor his heart quailed at the presence of danger."

"A most interesting young tiger, and a mighty handsome one," muttered Lillie aloud to herself in English. "The girl has certainly bewitched him. Good Lord!

what fools men are everywhere, about us poor giddy-pates!" Then she added aloud in French,—

"I cannot resist the temptation of playing my part in your little play, so you may depend upon me, and communicate the plan to Emineh Hanum, who I hope has courage enough to play hers, which is by far the hardest. When I ask her mother's permission to go to the bath with me, she will understand what I mean, and make her arrangements accordingly. But all other arrangements must be made by herself and her true friends," and she looked significantly at the young Turk. "Yet it is very certain that Emineh is not the girl to be able to fly alone, and your accompanying her would blast her reputation for ever. A girl educated and brought up in a harem is totally unfit for such a venture in every way. She would be caught immediately."

"Certainly," answered Selim, "but that has been already thought of. The French nurse will accompany her. She has the wit the courage and the devotion to her mistress to protect her, and take her safely to her father, now resident at Paris."

"You anticipate and answer all my doubts and objections," said Lillie. "'Peki,' as you always say. The game shall be played out, as far as I am concerned. I have no further difficulties to suggest."

The young man's face flushed with pleasure and admiration at the girl's courage and generosity. He rose from his chair, strode impulsively forward, seized the hand of Lillie, and bowing his haughty head, touched her fingers with his lips as respectfully as though rendering homage to an empress. "May your God and our Allah watch over, bless and protect you lady, for these noble words," he

said, " you have gained Paradise to-day
by befriending a helpless sister, and aiding
the weak. He will guard you both."

As though not trusting himself to say
more, and as if ashamed of the enthusiasm
so little in keeping with the ordinary
Turkish dignity and reserve, which
characterised his speech and demeanour,
Selim Pacha made a low prostration, and
rapidly strode out of the apartment,
leaving Lillie in a state of mind which she
herself found difficult to define. Yet with
the firm determination to keep the promise
which had been so strangely extorted from
her.

" Everybody says, I never will have
any common sense," she said to herself
meditatively, " and I begin to believe that
everybody is about right ! But I must
go through this thing, now that I have
promised, right or wrong. Poor little
Emineh ! "

CHAPTER XVII.

VISITING THE VALLEY OF THE HEAVENLY
WATERS—A RENCONTRE.

" SHALL we visit the Sweet Waters of Asia, Helen ? " asked Lillie. "Yanco tells me that Friday is the day on which to meet there all the ladies of the harem, who are not too lazy or too Frenchified to stay lolling on sofas, or divans rather, at home. We shall see some pretty scenery, and perhaps some pretty women, if there be a pretty woman out here except that lovely Emineh whom we saw at the Grand Pacha's the other day, and who proved to be the girl fished up out of the Bosphorus under our very eyes that memorable evening of the accident."

" Certainly," answered Helen, "I wonder we never thought of it before. It will be a nice row there in caiques, and we can pass a pleasant afternoon in seeing all the beauties of the Bosphorus, animate and inanimate. By all means let us go."

Accordingly the faithful Yanco made all the necessary arrangements, and the same afternoon the party were skimming the blue bosom of the Bosphorus in those frail caiques, which seem so peculiarly adapted to the country and the climate, as to make one indignant at the intrusion of the dirty smoky steamers, that now dispute possession with them.

It seemed to the girls like a trip through fairyland, as the frail caiques, impelled by the vigorous arms of the native boatmen, skimmed like swans over the water, the

panoramic views of both shores unfolding
new scenes of loveliness, as they glided
past. From the Golden Horn up to
Anatoli Hissar, where the Sweet Waters
are situated, a point halfway up to Buyukdere at the opening into the Black Sea,
the eye and mind of the traveller are filled
with beauty, distance lending enchantment
to the view of the villages nestling on
either bank, and diversified by the stately
imperial palaces and private *yalis*, wherein
the pachas take their *keff* or repose. The
scene on the water also is one of great
life and animation : since every possible
species of craft invented since the Ark find
place thereon. For while the " stately
ships come sailing from their shadows
under the hill," the little barque and laden
boats creep along the shore, and the
fishermen cast their nets with equal
clamorousness and success. Occasionally,

also, the caique of some high personage, pulled by six lusty rowers in gaudy uniform, shoots past you, and you see a pasty-faced fat contented-looking pacha reclining at ease on the cushions of the caique, like Homer's gods, careless of mankind.

Boatsful of veiled Turkish women of the middle or lower class may also be met, chattering together like magpies; and over all the arch of a cloudless sky, Italian in its depths of azure. At intervals on either shore may be seen, squatted near the bank, Turkish women in their bright raiments, like unto the ancient coat of Joseph, with their children gambolling round them. The mothers sit stolidly gazing out with expressionless eyes over the water, contrasting the frolicsome gaiety of the young ones. For the Turkish race resembles much in its ways the feline species

Nothing in nature can be more full of fun and frolic than a kitten, nothing more demure than a grown cat; and so it is with the Turk.

The palace of Beylerbey, in which the ill-fated French Empress Eugenie—whose fate recalls that of Marie Antoinette, save in tragic termination—was the Sultan's guest, rose up like a marble dream on the right hand as they rowed past. Then loomed up the ruined towers of Anatoli Hissar, constructed by the father of the conqueror Mohammed II., the first stride of the Turk towards his future capital.

Clustering beneath the frowning ruins of the grim old towers fast crumbling to decay, are the houses and huts of the Turkish village of Anatoli Hissar, a place of imprisonment where numerous captives perished from cruel treatment or neglect. Sad memories cluster around the " Black

Tower," as it was called in consequence. The marble palace of Sultan Abdul Medjid, one of the most lovely kiosks on the Bosphorus, smiles back to the grim old towers over the verdant meads which encompass it. The small freshwater river of Geuksoo, which gives its name to the place, winds in a curve for several miles around the plains and hills; and the valley formed by the river richly deserves from its picturesque beauty the poetic name the Turks have given it, " The Valley of the Heavenly Waters." It has even inspired poetry in the Turkish language, and a native bard has chaunted its praises.

After floating dreamily up the stream, spanned by rustic bridges in several places, the American party returned to the Bosphorus, and went on shore near the palace, which is situated close to the water's edge.

The two constructions are typical of the ancient and modern Turk. The soul of the one was in his fortifications and warlike enterprises, that of the other in his comfort and his pleasures: and Constantinople has proved his Capua.

Such thoughts impressed themselves on the minds of the pleasure pilgrims from a far distant land, as they surveyed the prospect; but their attention was soon diverted from the past to the present, and to the scenes around them on this pleasure-ground of the emancipated inmates of the harems, now making holiday with all the zest which the caged bird feels in its recovered liberty.

Very like a flock of glittering paroquets did they look, and quite as noisy, as squatted in groups on carpets spread on the grass under the shade of the trees, they babbled freely together, sipped

sherbets, ate sweetmeats and more solid
condiments, while the children romped
around them or ran over the green sward.
The brightness of the costumes, which
were of the liveliest colours, scarlets
purples greens silks and satins and
costly laces, with the flashing of jewels
and gems perceptible with each movement
of head or body, enhanced the gaiety of
the scene. The women of higher rank
were easily distinguishable, and kept themselves apart, after descending from the
telekas arabas or European carriages in
which they had been driving around this
Eastern Bois de Boulogne ; and their veils
could not conceal the regular features,
flashing eyes, and full proportions of these
lights of the harem, who seemed disposed to
repay with interest the inquisitive glances
of the strangers.

The charming prairie of the Asian

Sweet Waters, shaded by gigantic plane-
trees oaks and sycamores, presented
this moment the aspect of an earthly
paradise, peopled by multitudinous Eves—
whose infrequent Adams were obliged to
keep at a most respectful distance—since
it is against Moslem etiquette even for husband father or son or brother, to be seen
in company with, or address the female
members of his family in public.

Neither was it the habit of the Turkish
men to visit the Sweet Waters. The
masculine element was made up of Greeks
and Armenians, the former of whom
careered wildly about on horseback,
apparently in hope of attracting the
attention of the shrouded fair ones in
araba or on the green sward; and so
enacting the scenes in Byron's Giaour,
without their serious consequences or tragic
termination.

The carriages and conveyances of all kinds, crammed with their living freight, went round the drive as monotonously and succesively as at Hyde Park or the Prater, or any European promenade. The only difference was in the diversity of the conveyances, and the primitive character of some of them, as well as the Oriental costumes of their occupants. The arabas and telekas of the higher classes, as well as the oxen which drew them, were some of them very prettily decorated; but the open waggons with their canvas tops, carrying a dozen women, made no such pretensions to expense elegance or taste. Yet as elsewhere the lower class seemed to enjoy their recreation much more heartily than their more pampered sisters, and the shrill cries and laughter which arose from these long low waggons gave animation to the gathering, which otherwise would have been wanting.

Many of the high ladies seemed as
decorously dull as their class elsewhere,
and being more demonstrative and easy in
their manners than their western sisters,
and more addicted to showing their feelings
or emotions, did not scruple to yawn and
stretch themselves freely : in evidence of
being bored with their weekly repetition of
the same proceeding, which had lost all
interest and novelty to them, but which
fashion or health prescribed as a duty to
be gone through on each successive Friday
of the season : " since Stamboul has
its seasons," as well as London, Paris, or
Washington.

While the American girls, with their
escorts, were strolling over the flowery meads
of the Sweet Waters, and scrutinizing as far
as propriety permitted the various groups
of ladies congregated under the trees,
Helen suddenly stopped, and turning to

Lillie said, "Oh, Lillie, look at those Turkish ladies ! See under that grand old sycamore. Don't you recognize them ? and now they have recognized us ? It is Emineh with her mother, that stately-looking woman, who inspired us both with such awe and distrust at the same time, when we called there the other day at Scutari, and found out they were the heroines of the caique accident."

" Why certainly," replied Lillie, " Emineh's is not a face to be forgotten, nor for that matter is her mother's either. I suppose it is etiquette to approach and speak to them ? " All doubt on that point was soon put at rest by the Hanoum's rising up from her carpet, and beckoning the girls to approach, advancing a few steps towards them. The girls shook hands with the mother, who addressed them in perfect French. "How glad I am to see you, my dear girls; Emineh has been longing for another visit from you—why don't you come?"

"Well," said Lillie, "we do not know the etiquette of the East, but in our country we wait for our calls to be returned, before calling the second time."

"We Turkish ladies don't return calls, unless it is to a harem."

"But why don't you?" said Lillie.

"We are not allowed to go to a Giaour's house, for fear of meeting the men of the family; and as to visiting at an hotel it is impossible."

"That word 'allowed' would not suit me," said Lillie, "I always do what I myself think right, irrespective of the opinions of other people."

"In the East, my dear child, we must conform to the usages of the society in which we move," said the Hanoum with a little asperity.

" I suppose so," said Lillie, " but I can't understand why you don't all revolt against a played-out usage such as that."

" Played out, what does that mean ? " said the Hanoum.

" Why, that is an American expression for everything old, and no longer in use with our enlightened people."

" Well, dear, we won't discuss it, as it would take too long ; and I want to hear how you are enjoying our country."

" Pretty well," said Lillie, " but we are disappointed in so many things. For instance, we Americans from our earliest childhood are accustomed to read romances, naturally many are about the poetic East, so we expect so much that when we come here we are disappointed."

" In what way ? " said the Hanoum.

" For instance, the Oriental luxury of

the bath. I find them to be but dirty specimens of those we have at New Orleans."

"Indeed! Is it possible that you
have better baths there than we have
here ? "

"It is not only possible but certain.
Helen and I went to one in Stamboul which
they told us was the best, but we could
not stand the dirt."

" It was because you did not know how
to order your bath. Now, when we go, we
have a room specially prepared for us. I'll
tell you what you must do, come and take
your bath some Friday with us, and I
will show you Oriental luxury you have
never seen before."

" Thanks very much, madame, I shall be
delighted: and I am sure Helen will feel
equally pleased."

" What a sweet girl she seems to be ;
she and my daughter seem to be deeply

engaged in their conversation. Shall we join them ? "

" With pleasure," said Lillie.

So they walked across a green sward to where Helen and Emineh were talking in the most earnest manner. When she saw her mother coming towards them, she stopped her conversation, and became like a mute. Helen was so astonished at the sudden transformation, that she thought the girl was not well.

" What's the matter, dear ? "

" Oh, nothing, here comes mother ; don't you see her ? "

" Yes, but what of that ? "

" Hush ! not a word of what we have been saying. My dear friend, I depend on you."

Helen, who was a very innocent American girl, could not understand what her friend meant. Emineh had been telling her of her interview with Selim, and of her

father, but in a vague way. Lillie and the
Hanoum now joined them, so the conversation became general, Lillie telling
of her exploits in America and in Paris.
They laughed and enjoyed her conversation,
and the Hanoum was so fascinated with
Lillie that when she said to Emineh, in
her off-hand way, "Now my mind is
quite made up about having a real Turkish
bath before I go, and I intend to leave
Constantinople by the next mail or the one
after at latest, as I must meet my mother
in Paris on the 20th of next month. Will
you not be my Cicerone to the bath next
Friday?"

"Can you go, mamma?" said Emineh.

"I may be able to do so, but in any case
Mrs. H—— can take you, so I think you
can accede to your friend's wish." Lillie
and Emineh exchanged glances which it
was well the Hanoum did not see, as there

was joy and hope in them, that might have puzzled her. The Hanoum believed her daughter to be in complete ignorance of her birth; therefore she had no suspicions. She was pleased to give her the companionship of the European young ladies for she felt her daughter was dreadfully backward in all the usages of society. She therefore encouraged the intimacy, so far as it was in strict accordance with the Mussulman rules : for she was like all converts—more strict and particular than born Turks.

" At what hour shall we go to the bath ? " said Lillie.

" At about twelve o'clock," said Emineh.

" That is too late, much better be there at ten," replied Lillie, " and we can have an excellent luncheon put up at the hotel, and after we have been scrubbed, instead of taking your Turkish coffee, we shall eat a good substantial lunch ; I am sure by that time I shall be as hungry as a wolf."

" Oh, that would be very novel," said Emineh, " we could have our lunch in that little kiosk at the end of the garden."

" How charming," said Helen.

So it was arranged that the following Friday they should all meet at the bath at ten o'clock—no later.

" I am afraid you will have to excuse me," said the Hanoum, " for I never get up before ten : but I won't disappoint you girls. Madame Sourayan will accompany you."

Lillie espied Selim Pacha strolling along on the other side, so she jumped up and said good-bye to the Hanoum and Emineh, giving the latter's hand a very suggestive squeeze, which the other understood.

" Why are you in such haste ? " said the Hanoum.

" I see the General and our other friends are getting impatient to return, so we must not keep them waiting. We regret very much not being able to stay longer. We shall have a long row back to the bridge," answered Lillie.

The Hanoum and her daughter rose up to make their farewells, and it was agreed that on the ensuing Friday the visit to the bath at Galata Seraïl should be made; and so they parted, as the setting sun gilded the gently rippling river of the Heavenly Waters, and the grey old towers of Anatoli Hissar.

CHAPTER XVIII.

THE HAMMAMS AT GALATA SERAIL—THE FLIGHT.

THE public baths at Constantinople, of which in its various quarters there are about one hundred and fifty—cleanliness with Turkish women, as well as with Turkish men, being considered as akin to godliness—are better patronized than any local institution, coffee-shops not excepted.

On fixed days of the week certain of the better class of these are entirely devoted to women—and men excluded. On such reserved days they constitute the female clubs of Constantinople. Crowds of women spend the day there bathing, gossiping, exchanging the current scandal of their respective neighbourhoods, and feasting as well. For the better class take with them baskets of provisions, in which the famous Turkish sweets figure largely; and, if rumour does not belie them, the stimulants forbidden by the Prophet are not wanting to loosen the tongues of the "lights of the harem" on these occasions, when no masculine eye can pry on their proceedings. Many a reputation is lost in the confidential communications made on these club days, when the conversation is reputed to be as loose as the habits of the bathers, and tongues take holiday.

The mere pleasure of the bath itself, though doubtless great, is secondary to the social enjoyment so rarely accorded to Turkish women of the higher class. At Stamboul there are an immense number of public baths, resorted to by people of all classes and conditions, and varying in price, as they do in comfort and accommodation.

Attended by the inevitable eunuch, who tranquilly smokes and watches outside, while his fair charges are rioting within, the Turkish ladies greatly enjoy these occasional glimpses of partial liberty from supervision; and, like school-girls out of school, play rare pranks sometimes.

At Pera̅ the only large and fashionable public bath is that of Galata Seraïl, in the rear of the spacious gardens which front on the Grand Rue de Pera; about a hundred yards from the Grand Hotel. It is by far the largest best and cleanest to be found in any of the Christian parts of Constantinople, and is the resort of that more emancipated portion of the Turkish ladies who do not shun contact with Christian women, whether of Rayah or European origin, who also congregate there.

To this famous bath Lillie Hancock and her friend, chaperoned by an Armenian lady of their acquaintance, accompanied Emineh, doubly guarded by her old French nurse and the young eunuch specially assigned to her service, a few days after Lillie's colloquy with Selim Pacha.

They drove straight to the baths from Stamboul, the old woman entering the bath with them, the eunuch waiting on the carriage at the outer door; since they proposed spending only a few hours. not the entire day, in this improvised harem.

Emineh was very pale, but looked resolved; although, now that the hour of trial came, she felt the risk she was running, and the dread of a new and unknown future excited anxieties in her mind. How did she know, even if her evasion was successful, how this unknown father of hers might receive her ? What if he had transferred part of the indignation and contempt which he must naturally entertain for the mother to the daughter, her companion for so many years, known to him only as a little child ? Where then could she go and what could she do ? reared and trained as she had been, and as helpless as any Turkish woman would be in a similar situation ?

These thoughts naturally checked the exuberance of her feelings at the hope of a near escape from a hated captivity, and the realization of her long-cherished dream of freedom, and of rejoining the father whose image she so revered, stamped as it had been on her childish memory by

recollections of devoted affection. Her
companions also shared, though in a lesser
degree, in her anxieties ; for should the
proofs of their complicity in her abduction
become known or even be seriously suspected, it might affect the General's career
and prospects, or even lose him both ; since
no offence could be considered more grave
by the Turks than this. Nevertheless, in
spite of all doubts and fears, the programme
was strictly carried out as planned and
arranged. The French steamer was to
sail from its anchorage near the bridge at
two o'clock, and in a few minutes later
would be out at sea on her way to the
Dardanelles—Emineh's passage, as well as
that of her so-called aunt, had been taken
under French names—and once on board
the chances of their being arrested at the
Dardanelles, or suspected of being on the
Messageries steamer, were very small indeed.

A few minutes after the admission of the party of five bathers at the front door of the bathing-house, and after disrobing, Emineh was taken with a sudden faintness, which compelled her to be taken to a cooler room at the back of the building where there was fresh air. She pleaded so earnestly to be left alone there with her female attendant, that the Armenian lady and the two girls complied with her request. The three bathed with all the elaborateness of the Eastern system—were boiled roasted rubbed shampooed, curried down like horses, their joints cracked, their bodies first enveloped in soapsuds and then swathed in fleecy Turkish towels, then left half an hour to repose on divans, sipping finjans of coffee the while. After leisurely putting on their dresses again, the three ladies were informed that Emineh and her attendant had quitted the bath-house shortly after the others had left her, evidently by the back door, which opened on the side street, not on the Grand Rue de Pera; since on looking into the room a little later they had found it vacant.

"Very odd," said the Armenian lady, spitefully; "I must say not over polite, to treat us in this way? But what can you expect from these savages?" she added, shrugging her shoulders. "I hope, young ladies, you will excuse her rudeness: for poor thing! she knows no better."

"Oh certainly," said the ready Lillie, "I am only so glad that we have secured such a *chaperone* as you are, who understand the elegancies as well as the courtesies of life, and could not commit such a rudeness! Now, my dear madame, this place interests us both so wonderfully, that we should like to see something more of the way in which

Turkish ladies pass their time here, and with your explanations we can do so. We brought our lunch-basket filled with provisions from the hotel, for the purpose of making a day of it here, if you will allow us."

So saying the artful Lillie opened the lunch-basket, displaying a most appetizing luncheon, with the long necks of two champagne bottles peering above it, a beverage which all Levantine women specially affect, as well as their Turkish sisters who have made its acquaintance. Hence it was full two hours after the sailing of the Messageries steamer, before the Armenian lady and her two friends emerged from the bath-house; and then they enlisted her attention so entirely, that she did not remark that the pacha's carriage, with the eunuch perched on the box, still stood near the side walk : particularly since for the sake of the shade at that broiling hour, the coachman had taken it down the side street under the trees, expecting a summons when needed.

What had happened in the interval was this. A few minutes after being left alone, the old French woman produced a bundle from under her cloak, containing two European costumes of a very common description, but with two thick green veils for the bonnets. Hastily slipping them on, and making another bundle of their own garments, the two women watched their opportunity, when all the bath attendants were engaged, slipped out of the back door where a hack awaited them, on which was perched a man in sailor's dress, and closing the blinds drove rapidly away, until they reached the landing-place at Tophane. There the sailor paid and dismissed the coachman, placed the two women in a row-boat, jumped in himself, and all three were rowed over to the Messageries steamer, puffing and snorting in token of speedy departure. Twenty minutes later the steamer was off, and two female passengers more added to her list, whose berths had been secured days before.

Letters received from Europe some weeks later, addressed to Helen, gave tidings of the safe arrival of the fugitives, and their warm reception by the astonished and delighted father, whose affection knew no bounds.

Emineh was happy for a time, in the fulfilment of her dreams; but the fair fugitive soon discovered that a new presence persistently obtruded itself on her maiden thoughts, and more than rivalled even her restored father's image in her heart. It was that of the young Turkish pacha, who had twice been her rescuer. But maiden pride kept her silent, and for many years he made no sign.

Years later, when Selim Pacha had become military attaché at Paris, their acquaintance was renewed under more favourable auspices, and Emineh finally became the wife of a Turkish pacha after all; but of one so thoroughly Europeanized as to treat her not as a soulless toy, but as a companion counsellor and friend.

As Selim's agency in her rescue never was known, and her relatives at Constantinople forgave her after her marriage, no evil consequences followed her flight— and her home on the banks of the Bosphorus was a happy one for many years.

CHAPTER XIX.

A PACHA OF THE OLD SCHOOL.

ALL along the curving shore of the Golden
Horn on the Stamboul side, but on the
heights distant from the water and overlooking it, with grand vistas of the
surrounding country, are to be found
the palaces of the pachas who have
enjoyed Imperial favour. These constitute for the time being the aristocracy
or court circle, in this most democratic of
despotisms, where the rise and fall of
ministers and favourites are as rapid and
dramatic, as any which characterized the
far-famed court of the Grand Duchess of
Gerolstein.

From the bridges, or from the Golden Horn itself you observe those large buildings, surrounded by lofty walls shutting in great gardens, but there is nothing palatial in their external appearance; and neither the approaches to, nor the arrival at any of these residences, indicate that you are about visiting the great ones of the earth. For the way is long rough and filthy beyond imagination, through tortuous lanes rather than streets, over disjointed stones, for most of the route. One peculiarity of the life of Stamboul is the entire desertion of the streets after dark and throughout the night, when the place is as silent and devoid of human presence, as the streets of disentombed Pompeii. There are no watchmen, no police prowling around to make night hideous by the striking of their long sticks on the pavement, as do the Bekjes of

K

Galata and Pera. No such precautions
are necessary in a city, where to be abroad
at night would of itself indicate a felonious
intent, and rouse the neighbourhood
against the suspicious prowler. The dogs
too, which throughout the day are so gentle
and inoffensive, are the reverse during
the hours of darkness; and constitute a
most efficient patrol, falling in troops on
any venturesome intruder upon their several
beats, who is not recognized. It would be
worth the life of any Christian or stranger,
to venture at night into the more secluded
streets of Stamboul for this reason alone:
or even into many of those inhabited by
Greeks or Armenians.

Hence the remarkable absence of crimes
of violence or burglaries, in a populous city
full of needy people, unlighted, unguarded,
with valuables stowed away in security in
small wooden shops, protected only by

rotten wooden shutters, whose owners are tranquilly sleeping at home.

A great city whose scavengers and police are dogs, and homeless vagabond dogs picking up a precarious livelihood from Frank and Turkish charity, is a curious fact in the history of this nineteenth century. But such is the case at Stamboul—although civilization, in the shape of tramways and horse-cars, has penetrated into its narrow and filthy streets and for many miles inside and outside of its walls.

The daily lives and habitudes of this four-footed patrol, living in communities, and under fixed forms of government, with territorial limits strictly assigned and recognized by unwritten canine law, have been so often described by the multitudinous writers of travels in the East, that it would be superfluous to repeat that old story.

But their exercise of police functions

K 2

is a fact which seems to have escaped the
notice of travellers; it never having been
the habit of the dragomen to make noc-
turnal excursions into a city, where everything is shut up at dark, and everybody
retires into the bosom of his family, or at
least into his sleeping-place, from which
he does not emerge until the ensuing morn.
But a small portion of Stamboul has
been opened by tramway.

From the Galata bridge you wind your
crooked way in a crazy hack through
these lanes, which are shut in by the shops
of the small traders or artisans, Turks
or Christian Rayahs of Greek or Armenian origin, but almost undistinguishable
from their Moslem masters in appearance,
and almost as Oriental in their modes of
life. These shops or restaurants present
the same uniform aspect of squalor,
poverty and filth; and hungry wolfish-
looking dogs, and neglected children, laden

men and donkeys, dispute the narrow
street, which seldom boasts even a small
strip of side-walk. The sights sounds
and smells which accompany you are pain-
fully Oriental, and the howling of the
itinerant vendors of fruits and vegetables,
mixed with the whine of the beggars,
pursues you like a discordant chorus,
which even the rattling and creaking of
your vehicle cannot drown.

Over these break-neck roads, General
Prescott, with two of his American aides, was
jolted one morning, to pay an early visit to
one of the Grand Marshals of the Empire at
his Stamboul residence. For this magnate
had no less than three, one at Stamboul,
another at Beckishtach near the Sultan's
palace, the third within the precincts of
the park of Yildiz, the royal residence.

Reaching a large iron gate in a high
white wall, over the top of which was to
be seen the roofs of a lofty mansion, the

latticed windows in one wing of which indicated the harem, the carriage stopped, and the General and his suite passed into a courtyard which led to a dilapidated-looking old building, the former dwelling-house, overlooked by the new palace behind it.

Mounting up some dirty and well-worn old steps, the party was ushered into a waiting-room in the old building, whose only furniture consisted of ancient divans which had seen much and hard service. A rusty old iron stove filled one corner of the room, and the windows had apparently not been washed for many years; so that you could see but dimly through them into a green and spacious garden.

A servant in shabby and not over-clean Eastern costume, brought in small cups of coffee, not Oriental *fingans* or egg-shell cups as in Egypt, but with saucers, and cigarettes, of both of which the guests partook while waiting for their host. In the corner of the reception-room was a small cot-bed, on which some one had evidently been sleeping : and some garments were carelessly thrown upon it.

Such was the entrance to the palace of this grand pacha—one of the richest and highest, in the ,empire—and the strangers were astonished beyond measure with this, their first experience, of Oriental luxury and comfort.

In a short time however, a messenger came to announce that the Grand Marshal would receive them : and one of his aides, an educated young Turk who spoke French like a Frenchman, dressed in a handsome uniform, led the way up another flight of steps into the new palace beyond, in which the pacha resided : informing the guests as they went that it was intended shortly to pull down the old building, and apologizing for its rusty condition.

The apartment into which they were now conducted was in striking contrast with the one they had just left, for it was fresh spacious and crammed with the newest and most gorgeously gilded French furniture and upholstery. There was nothing Oriental in or about it, except its occupant, a withered old man perched up on a gilded arm-chair, dressed in full uniform of a most gorgeous description, with a red fez cap on his head.

He rose up, came forward and shook hands with the General and his officers, motioned them to be seated, and re-seated himself, fixing his bright, black bead-like eyes inquisitively upon his visitors. He was a small spare man, whose face was seamed with innumerable wrinkles, with a beak like that of a bird of prey, and a sinister and cruel expression about the firmly compressed lips. Although a very

old man, there was nothing either in his
face or movements to indicate any of the
infirmities of age. He looked as tough
dry and hard as a winter apple. Compre-
hending no foreign language, he had to
speak through an interpreter, and the
aide-de-camp already mentioned performed
that function for him.

The conversation was of the simplest
and most disjointed kind, and the guests
felt relieved, when the pacha proposed to
show them over his gardens, which were
very extensive and well-kept, with a
miniature lake, modelled on that of the
Bois de Boulogne, in one portion of them.
There was also a private mosque inside of
the garden, although the pacha's life
and history would prove him to have been
anything but a very pious person. Yet all
the appliances were there. The stables,
containing a dozen horses for his own and

his son's use, were very spacious, and contained specimens of the Arab and European, as well as of the Turkish breeds. Adjoining these stables was a kiosk, in which a fountain played perpetually, and glass windows gave light and air to it on all sides. Here, squatted on his divan, smoking his nargileh, the pacha doubtless felt more at ease and passed more of his time, than in the gorgeously-decorated imitation European reception-room. Here again coffee was served, and the pacha warming up a little, gave his guests some reminiscences of his very eventful life. For he had a history, this old pacha, dating far back with the days when Mehemet Ali of Egypt menaced the throne of the Sultan; and actively continued in Montenegro, Egypt, and Turkey, down to the moment when these strangers saw him.

There was something in his aspect and

ways which recalled the portrait of
Mehemet Ali, something of the tiger-cat
and of the fox blended together, the face
of a strong wilful unscrupulous man,
who looked to the end to be accomplished,
and ready to compass it by force or
fraud as circumstances might require,
without being troubled with moral or any
other scruples.

In the suppression of the Montenegrin
revolt against the Sultan, he showed great
strategy and great cruelty, and his name
was long a terror there. When sent as
commissioner to Egypt, when Arabi Pacha
first commenced his rebellious movements
against the young Khedive Tewfik, the
grim old man proposed the speedy suppression of the rebellion, by cutting off its
head ; and promised to undertake the job
of enticing and hanging Arabi, if approved
of by that prince.

Arabi was cowed and disheartened by
his presence and character, which he well
knew, until learning the refusal of Tewfik, he took heart of grace, defied him, and
pursued the path which led to his tem-
porary dictatorship the Anglo-Egyptian
war and his exile to Ceylon. With a
more unscrupulous man on the Egyptian
throne the old pacha would soon have
stamped out the nascent rebellion, and
have made a victim of its author. The
old pacha, though courteous in manner to
those he liked, had none of the suppleness
or suavity of the ordinary Turk. He
spoke little, and that little was short
sharp and decisive. His very humour
was of an excessively practical description,
as was his mind. He greatly admired the
Americans as a practical people, and had
adopted several of their inventions on his
grounds and in his gardens. Of culture

he had none, of education scarcely any,
having been self-educated in the school of
the palace, where he had charge of the
Sultan's son and possible heir. He was a
self-taught soldier also, but his thorough
knowledge of the character of the Eastern
people stood him in stead of military
instruction, and he had a natural taste and
aptitude for fighting and diplomatizing.
He was reputed to have great influence at
the palace, and his love of money, originally
great, increased with his years, until
he was reputed to be one of the richest
pachas in the empire. A very old man,
his skinny hands still tenaciously clung to
power and to money ; and with innumerable
enemies he still continued to baffle and
beat them all, and hold his place near the
Sultan's ear, wielding an influence second
to that of none, although his master
knew his character thoroughly, and

closely watched while he apparently con-
fided in him.

The son and aide-de-camp of the old
pacha were two good specimens of the third
generation of the present day. The former,
already a promising young officer, though
but nineteen years of age, was really an
accomplished young man, though he had
never travelled abroad. His two predomi-
nating tastes were for horses and for literature. He neither drank nor smoked, nor
practised the other vices common to the
Turks. His time was spent in study or
on horseback. In his capacious overcoat
pockets he carried copies of the French
classics, such as Moliere and his compeers,
and was fond of conversing about them.
His bearing though manly was modest,
and the fresh simplicity and charming
frankness of his manner were in striking
contrast with the cunning and reticence of

his father, of whom, however, he was the
special favourite. He seemed a born
patrician in all respects, and all the
pampering he had received had failed to
spoil him, or corrupt the ingenuousness of
his nature. The aide-de-camp was of a
different type, a powerfully-built bronzed
man of thirty, who had seen service in the
war with Russia, and promoted to the
grade of major for gallantry in the field.
He too spoke and read French with
fluency, and frequented the French
theatre to enjoy their sparkling comedies ;
but his tastes were more military than
literary, and he was fond of European
society. Neither of these young men
seemed to have the slightest tinge of
fanaticism, and were exponents of the
most promising class in Turkey. But
unhappily they were isolated specimens,
and but very few indeed resembling them

were ever encountered by General Prescott and his comrades, during their term of service in Turkey.

These young men were very frank and fearless in expressing their opinions, and exposing the corruption and favouritism of their superiors; partly because the old pacha could not understand the drift of their discourse, and partly because they thought they could safely do so with these American republicans.

The old pacha said little, but smoked incessantly, and seemed to think Turkey the best of all possible worlds, and himself the best of all possible pachas. The questions he put about America displayed clearly the immense depth of his ignorance in relation to that country, its people, its progress and its future. In this respect he was on a par with the great bulk of his brother pachas, whose horizon is bounded

by the limits of their own country. The
old pacha was evidently proud of his new
palace, and took his guests over the
selamlik or men's apartments; the sacred
precincts of the harem, occupying the
other wing, of course not being profaned
by the masculine foot of any one, save
of the master of the house and his
eunuchs. Suite after suite of spacious
and splendidly decorated apartments, for
his own use and that of his sons, was
exhibited to the visitors, furnished in the
most lavish French style of decoration,
with costly mirrors, gilt chairs covered
with brocade, and curtains stiff with
embroidery. No expense was spared in
the fitting up, which must have cost a
prince's ransom. Yet the old pacha has
the reputation of loving money more than
anything else, and his private habits are
said to be avaricious, while his tradesmen

have always a hard fight for their bills. This strange blending of profuseness with parsimony, splendour with squalor, covetousness with ostentation, forms a marked element of Oriental character; especially with the elder generation of Turks. The younger generation is reckless in expenditure, and understand how to spend judiciously at the same time. The improvements made in the spacious gardens, covering many acres, showed that old as he was the pacha was a progressive man. He had introduced one of the American windmill waterwheels for the irrigation of the grounds, and had a miniature Bois de Boulogne at one end of the garden, with a rustic bridge and lake.

The East is the land of gardens, where the bulbul still chants his passionate love songs to the rose, and the uneducated and otherwise unsentimental Turk seems to enjoy nature, far more than his more refined western brother. The grim old pacha was the last man one would have suspected of enjoying or appreciating such environments. Yet he sat among his roses, and listened to his nightingales, with a serene satisfaction which softened his rugged lineaments into the semblance of sentiment.

It was long past midday, and as no more substantial refreshments had been tendered to the visitors, than the perpetually recurring coffee and cigarettes, they thought it high time to conclude their visit. After an interchange of multitudinous salaams and salutations on both sides, they returned to their hotel, where an ample breakfast filled the aching void caused by the Barmecide feast of this pacha of the old school—type of a vanishing species.

CHAPTER XX.

A PACHA OF THE NEW SCHOOL.

THE heights of Chamliza at Scutari, on
the Asiatic side of the Bosphorus, command perhaps the most comprehensive
and picturesque view of the surrounding
seas, and the wonderful scenery which
frames them in, of any point on that side
of the Bosphorus. It is the favourite site
on which the pachas of the new school
have pitched their residences, blending the
old habitudes of the East with the new
ones of the West; but keeping up, for
obvious reasons, many of the modes of life
and habitudes of the Mussulman population and faith, especially as regards their
domestic life.

For never was the jealous pride of the oriental more keenly acute in everything which relates to foreign interference, than it has been since the latest Sultans learned, by personal inspection of Europe, how far in advance of the East the West had become; and how great was the danger from the encroachments of civilized ideas and civilized policy of the Franks, if ever their patient oxen,—the Ottoman people—should learn to appreciate the difference, or the contrast between the two systems.

The Turkish pacha, or his secretaries, who have spent a few years in Europe, and learned to compare the two systems respectively prevailing in the East and West, are naturally looked on with jealousy and suspicion, both by the Sultan himself, and by the fanatical old Mussulman—the cardinal doctrine of whom is hatred of the Giaour (Infidel) and all his works.

Hence the reforming element in Turkey
has a most delicate and difficult part to
play, in not offending national suscepti-
bilities, or giving even plausible pretexts
to the old palace ring of retrogrades and
thieves, who live on plunder, to accuse
them of acting or advising in European
interests. This enormously increases the
difficulty of making any real improvements
inside or outside of the palace, which
really is the fountain of all practical work,
or changes of any kind; since without
Imperial Irade or order, nothing ever
is done in any department of the Government, of any practical value.

Let us now visit one of the leading
pachas of the new school, in company with
General Prescott and his staff. Crossing
the Bosphorus from the Galata bridge to
Scutari, or taking the longer route to the
depôt of the Haïdar Pacha Railway, within

twenty-five or thirty minutes you find yourself landed in Asia on the shores of Scutari,
where most good Mussulmen, wherever
they may dwell, prefer being buried; and
which is at once the chosen spot selected
by the True Believer in which to live, or
to be peacefully interred.

The day selected by the American
general and his suite was well chosen. It
happened to be the first day of the Turkish
spring—a few days later but corresponding
with our May day—and the whole Turkish
population, male and female, of the better
class, from Scutari Stamboul and the
adjacent places poured out to the plain
of Haïdar Pacha, in carriages, on foot
or by steamer, to make a holyday on
the vast plain which surrounds that place ;
pitching tents, and occupying every square
foot of space left vacant, to make themselves more comfortable.

Bands of music, both Turkish and European, discoursed excellent melodies at
intervals ; while coupés and carriages containing loads of Turkish veiled beauties of
the higher class, with veils so transparent
as to enhance not hide the beauties of the
face and form they were supposed to conceal from the vulgar gaze, formed a procession similar to that of Hyde Park, along the
crowded way ; giving the pedestrians a fair
chance of surveying their beauties, now no
longer protected by savage eunuch, prompt
to use the sword on the slightest provoca-
tion real or supposed, as formerly. Toiling
and groaning after these Parisian or English
carriages come the creaking native araba,
or waggon drawn by oxen with gilded
caparisons, whose long benches are filled
by Turkish matrons and maidens, sump-
tuously arrayed, but with the invariable
yashmac and feridge shrouding their

mature or budding charms more com-
pletely, than the gauzy pretences of the
higher class.

Over the whole wide space for miles
might be seen the moving mass of human
beings; tents being erected on slight
eminences, with refreshment booths,
affording coffee sweets lemonades or
nargilés; but no intoxicating beverages
of any description—a lesson Europe
well might learn at her public gather-
ings.

The vast multitude was not exclusively
composed of Turks, although they constituted the great majority, but of all the
other varied nationalities composing the
mixed population of Constantinople—including the Greek Christians, whose *fête* of
St. George happened to fall on the same
day, and who made it a general holyday
for that reason. A better-tempered and

more orderly crowd could be found in no
country on the earth; and the presence of
the policeman seemed totally unnecessary,
although here and there you might descry
one.

Probably the absence of intoxicating
drinks, may have much to do with the
invariably orderly conduct of an Eastern
crowd.

The only sounds heard, were the cries
of the itinerant vendors advertising their
wares and refreshments, and the indescrib-
able hum arising from distant human
voices, like the buzzing of bees in swarm-
ing time. The gay babble of busy tongues
from those nearer added to the animation
of the scene. Merry-go-rounds and other
cheap modes of amusing the public were
not wanting, and the grown children of
mature age seemed to enjoy these sports as
much as their juniors.

Every class and condition seemed to be represented on this occasion, from the high lady of the harem, with her gossamer veil, leaning back in her coupé, and curiously peering out on humanity from her Kohl-stained glittering eyes, to the day-labourer, trudging along on foot in his weekday dress of shreds and patches, and the professional beggar exhibiting his deformities as an appeal to the charitable, with swarms of middle-class Turks Greeks Armenians and Europeans : and the cafés drove a roaring trade in supplying their simple wants.

Leaving this animated scene behind, the Americans took a carriage, and drove for about two miles along a broad road which gave picturesque views of the sea and surrounding scenery, from the heights which dominated the shore. Palaces, houses and hovels were sprinkled along

the road-side. Among others an old and
disused palace, with high walls and spacious
gardens surrounding it, the former resort
of Abdul Aziz, the present Sultan's pre-
decessor. The sentries were still at the
gate, but the place was and would remain
uninhabited, save by the slaves and
gardeners who took charge of it.

At length they arrived at Chamliza, and
at the rambling building or palace occupied by the pacha, for whom their visit
was intended: a very pacha of pachas,
a Grand Marshal, one of the most prominent men of the empire, but holding no
political position, although the intimate
and trusted adviser of the Sultan, who
probably did not himself distinctly know
whether he loved or feared him most.

They found the pacha in his selamlik,
as the men's side of the house is ever
styled.

A tall stalwart man, with sharp, clear-cut features, closely-clipped brown beard and moustache, a fair blonde complexion, blue eyes, with bold frank expression meeting yours directly, unlike the usual Turkish habitude, which is to avoid the eye of the interlocutor, and a wonderful fluency of speech, whether in French or in Turkish, his foreign travel having quite European-ized him.

His dress, a costly cloth wrapper lined with fur, coming down to his slippered feet, for he was in demi-toilette, for which he apologized—and sitting *à la Turque* upon a broad divan, playing chess with one of his friends squatted opposite to him.

On his head was the red fez, sole symbol of his Eastern nationality, but this he occasionally removed, displaying a head covered with closely-cropped dark brown hair.

When he rose to receive and greet his guests—all the Turks present rising at the same time—his athletic and graceful movements indicated the powerful and agile frame his loose wrapper covered ; and the grace of his gestures was equally significant of the courtier, as well as the soldier.

The sitting-room or selamlik, in which the pacha entertained his guests, was Oriental only from its divans of Persian carpetings, and the rich Turkish rugs covering the floor. A grand glass chandelier with thirty lustres hung in the middle of the apartment ; under it a richly carved table of Italian handiwork, of great beauty and price, on which was placed an equally rich and rare *jardinière* filled with flowers. Several books in Turkish and French were strewn over the table, mingled with cartridges, explosive and otherwise, and other objects pertaining to the chase. On a fanciful stand supported by three foils for legs, cigarettes and matches were placed: and in the corner a handsome stove supplied the place of the ancient mangal or brazier which sufficed for the pacha's progenitors. The old was evidently giving place to the new, in as far as the furniture was concerned; but among the native guests none, save the pacha, spoke or understood any language but his own, except an Armenian secretary who wrote the pacha's correspondence at his dictation. There were old Turks, middle-aged Turks, and young Turks, but they clung to their own speech and their own writing, and to their own thinking as well, even under the shadow of the great reforming pacha whose adherents they all were.

In a few well-chosen words he greeted

his guests, welcoming them to the country,
and expressing his personal pleasure at
seeing them at his house, where they
would ever be welcome; and turning to
his friends announced who they were
and what their mission was. Much salaam-
ing and saluting followed this introduction.

The pacha had made his reputation, by
his daring and gallantry in the war with
Russia, and was Grand Marshal of the
Palace and high in the confidence of his
sovereign, and he greeted General Prescott as a brother in arms, giving most
interesting accounts of his own campaign,
with much vivacity, but without any personal boastfulness.

Breakfast was announced, and the
pacha insisted on his guests remaining
to partake of it with him. The breakfast
was Oriental in its character and cookery,

but served in European style, with all the European appointments as perfect as possible.

By the side of each foreign guest wine glasses were placed, and French wines provided. Most of the Turks drank water only, two or three indulged in beer, —the prophet's prohibition being wine! but with the higher class generally, even that prohibition is now " more honoured in the breach than in the observance."

Motioning his newly-arrived guests to be seated on the ottomans which occupied all sides of the room, the pacha subsided again on his own divan, with the grace and ease of a tiger-cat; touched an electric bell-knob set in the wall, when small *fingans,* or egg-shell cups of steaming coffee, together with cigarettes, were promptly presented to the latest guests, as well as to the host—an invariable preliminary to conversation in a Turkish household. His father, a venerable man of eighty years of age, but still vigorous and in possession of all his faculties, and filling a high position in the court of the Sultan, was seated near the pacha. But he, unlike his son, could speak nor understand no language but his own, although he had visited England and France in the suite of a former Sultan many years before. The other persons to the number of half a dozen, were relatives friends or retainers of the pacha; for a Turkish magnate always has attached to his house and person a string of retainers, as long as that which formerly constituted the "tail" of an ancient Scottish chieftain.

The dishes were chiefly composed of chopped-up meats and vegetables, ending with a huge platter of roast lamb, followed by a great variety of sweet dishes.

The good old Eastern habit, of presenting each guest an ewer and basin to wash the hands before partaking of the meat,—like the old Chibouque and Turkish dress—has been dispensed with now in Turkey. All the guests wore the Frank dress, the servants only retaining the eastern costume.

In fact, the *mélange* of Eastern and Western habitudes was most curious; and the oriental appetite surprised the new comers, the Turks being very heavy feeders, in compensation probably of their abstinence from the fluids which wash down the viands of the west.

The conversation was naturally as mixed as the other component parts of the banquet; but the pacha kept the ball of conversation actively going all the time, in French Turkish Italian Persian and other languages, first addressing himself to one set of his convives, and then to

the other, occasionally indulging in an
English phrase for the benefit of his
Western guests, since he had picked up a
little English in his visits to London.
Among the guests was a melancholy-
looking furrowed-faced man, prematurely
old, with bowed frame and grey hair,
wearing an old uniform, but with a
restless glittering eye denoting intense
mental activity and anxiety. After the
breakfast was over the pacha told
his guests the story of this man—one
very characteristic of the country. He
had been colonel of Engineers in the
Turkish army, with a fatal gift for inventions, in which he was eternally experi-
menting. Among other things, he
invented some explosive bombs, which he
asked permission to exhibit before His
Majesty the Sultan. The consequence
was, his dismissal from the army, his loss

of rank and pay, and imprisonment for
three years! some one having whispered
that he meditated a murderous assault upon
His Majesty with these infernal machines
of his invention. The poor man emerged
from his imprisonment utterly broken in
health and fortune, living in the midst
of the wrecks of his inventions, in a
dilapidated old house; yet still full of
the fire of the inventor, and hoping
against hope to utilize some of them.
The rewards of inventors elsewhere, with
a few notable exceptions, have not usually
been very great; but in this case, even
the worse than proverbial lot has fallen on
this Turkish aspirant to rank among the
distinguished inventors.

The pacha had retired for a few minutes
before breakfast, to dress for that meal, and
appeared in his undress uniform, which set
off his manly figure to perfection.

Sending for a gun, used by him in bear-hunting, (for which he had a passion), he held it out at arm's-length with one hand, a feat which no one present could imitate. Then, passing down into the garden, he caused an iron plate of an inch thick to be set up as a target, and, with an explosive ball, penetrated through the iron and deep into the wall behind it, showing the terrible force of the weapon and its charge.

The recoil of the gun was sufficient to knock down a man of ordinary strength; but only slightly shook the sinewy bulk of the pacha, when the explosion took place. He then gave an animated narrative of some of his hunts, especially lauding the courage and skill of a friend and neighbour, then present, who had entered the cave of a wounded bear, and killed it in a hand-to-hand fight.

For the pacha like Nimrod is a mighty hunter, and his most intimate friends are those who share the same tastes.

Like all other Turks, whether Europeanized or not, the pacha strictly kept up the Harem system, although rejoicing in but one wife. The children, to the number of eight, fine fresh chubby-looking creatures,—the boys preserving that wonderful Oriental solemnity which seems inborn in all Turkish children,— solemnly marched in to kiss their father's hand, and those of his guests.

But the household seen' by guests was all masculine, and while the social life of the East undergoes no change, it were idle to expect any great alteration in the character or the habits of the population. Since it is the home-life which forms the child, who as the poet Wordsworth declares is ever " The father of the man," the early training of the harem, among ignorant women, can never be subsequently effaced by any amount of foreign travel or foreign education; and until Islam renounces her religion and social system, her offspring will continue substantially the same.

The conversation at the table and afterwards was naturally of the most mixed and miscellaneous kind. Much curiosity was manifested by the Turkish portion of the company in America and Americans, and very curious were the questions asked.

The pacha however, seemed to know a great deal about these matters ; and General Prescott and he had much conversation on the military attitude of the Powers, and of Turkey respectively.

But the difficulty of anything like a connected conversation under such circumstances can easily be conceived.

After more coffee and cigarettes, inspection of arms of various kinds, and of
maps and plans of strategic positions, the
American party took their leave, escorted
courteously to the steps by the pacha, all
of his guests rising up and saluting them
as they left the room.

The return was by the other route—
over break-neck stony roads, past grave-
yards, palaces hovels cultivated and
uncultivated fields, down the hill to the
landing-place at Scutari, three miles distant, where they found the steamer.

CHAPTER XXI.

HELEN'S CHOICE.

THE days and months rolled rapidly by, and time trampled under his remorseless foot as he hurried by, many a heart, many a hope, and many a life, fresh fair and full of promise before his passing. Lillie and her party had long left Constantinople, and returned to a home, which if not so picturesque, was yet devoid of the filth, material and moral, which frames in Constantinople. Old Celia, pining for the " old plantation folks " in South Carolina, with a love and longing surpassing that of the Swiss for his mountain home, had wasted away slowly but surely, and now

slept under the solemn cypresses in the
Protestant grave-yard at Scutari. So
that Helen was left very solitary and very
sad, finding no congenial associates among
her new acquaintances in the Europeo-
American society at Constantinople. The
American colony was almost exclusively
composed of missionaries, or religious
people devoted to educational pursuits,
with whom the Southern girl had no sym-
pathy; and her father's duties prevented
her seeing much of him. So the field was
clear for the wooing of the young Armenian, and he availed himself of and profited by his opportunities. In her pride of
the family old Celia had boasted much of
the Prescott property at home, and inspired
in the young man's mind the idea that her
young mistress was, or would some day be
a great heiress; scoffing at " dem Californy
gold people " as almost paupers in com-

parison, whose wealth might any day
cease with the end of the gold vein in
their mines. Hence the young man, who
had hesitated as to which of the two
should have the transferance of his facile
affections, decided to press his suit on
Helen, so as to become possessed of the
Southern plantation of which old Celia
talked so much; while, at the same time,
the girl's fresh young beauty captivated
his senses and his imagination, contrasting
her, as he did, with the Armenian women
of his acquaintance. To the general and
his American friends, as well as to Helen
herself, he presented only the smoother
and more attractive traits of his character
and conduct, hiding the seamy side carefully from their cognizance; and the
ignorance of the Americans as to his
antecedents, and very slight acquaintance
with the residents, prevented their getting

any outside information, which might have enlighted them as to his real character and habits.

As to Helen, she was living in the Fool's Paradise, formed by young girls during their first attachment; and would have believed no evil of her admirer, even had such been communicated to her. To her he was the embodiment of her visions of romance, the realization of " Love's young dream," and his Oriental origin and surroundings enhanced the poetry of the situation. When General Prescott's eyes were opened to the actual condition of affairs, his surprise and disapproval took such very strong methods of demonstration, as to help rather than hurt his daughter's lover in her estimation. For he went too far, and was unjust in his denunciations of the young man's character and motives, of which he could produce no proofs; thus awakening the sympathies of the generous young girl.

Finding he could produce no change of sentiment in the girl by his reasoning, he invoked the aid of his paternal authority to forbid their meeting or corresponding, with the usual happy result of increasing the appetite of both for those forbidden communications. Finally the fond father saw to his dismay that his daughter's health and spirits began to fail under her probation, and although always dutiful and kind, her manner had become less demonstratively affectionate than was her wont. Her mother had died of consumption, and now the hereditary taint seemed to be exhibiting itself in the daughter. The form grew thinner, the face less round, a hectic spot appeared on the cheek, and a hacking cough shook the slight frame day and night. The stout heart of the old general, which had bravely withstood the buffets of adverse fortune, in the loss of property of home and of " the Cause " in which he had staked both, that heart which had concentrated all the paternal affection which had once been shared by many children on ,this sole ewe lamb which Providence had left him ; quailed under this new calamity, and its possible consequences to his only surviving child.

So he determined to save her imperilled health and life at the expense of himself, and reluctantly consented that his daughter should wed the Armenian, with an instinctive dread of the results of such an union. He was rewarded by the immediate restoration of his daughter's health and gaiety. The rose came back again to her cheek, and the brightness to her eye ; and the poor father knew not whether to feel more pleased or pained at the transformation ; whether to smile or to sigh over the selfishness of his child, though he well knew the instinct of the young, in man as with other animals, to desert the parent nest when the parental protection is no longer a necessity. As a matter of course, Helen was introduced to the family and the relations of the young Armenian, who marvelled much at their kinsman's taste in his selection, but consoled themselves with the idea of the rich dower she was supposed to bring with her; Levantine gossip having greatly swollen even the well-meant exaggerations of poor old Celia as to her mistress' fortune.

The wedding ceremony had to be a triple one, in consequence of the different nationality and religious creed of the contracting parties, so as to make the marriage a valid one. In the first place the consular authority had to be invoked, and the civil contract made there before that Official, in the presence of witnesses ; a half-religious half-legal celebration. Then came firstly the formal religious marriage ceremony at the chapel of the English Embassy at Pera, after which the ceremony according to the Armenian rite, at the Armenian Church in the rear of the Grand Hotel.

The Armenian Church at Constantinople is divided into two distinct branches, the Roman Catholic, and the Gregorian or Orthodox: and bitter is the sectarian hatred between the two. The Latin branch is supported by France,—the Orthodox by Russia.

The old rites and usages of the primitive Eastern Church, with a large infusion of Oriental customs, are still observed in the one, while in the other the formula of the Roman Church everywhere is observed. Under the old Armenian rite the cercmony was a most elaborate affair—as it still is under the Greek.

The bride was first taken to the bath, on the Friday preceding the marriage, and the wedding took place on the ensuing Monday. On Saturday and Sunday musicians were called into the house of the bride's parents, and rich and poor invited to partake of the feasts prepared in honour of the coming occasion. At the wedding dinner the bride and groom sat side by side. After dinner the wedding gifts, together with the wedding garments,—which must first receive the benediction of the priest, as well as the presents—were brought out and exhibited : the bridegroom with his friends escorting them to the door of the bride's house.

The betrothal was made, not by a ring, but by the presentation to the lady of a gold cross from the future husband, which had been obtained from the priest, and blessed by the Church.

The ceremony commenced by the priest putting the question to the two, " *Chiosus topalus cabullus ?*"—" Blind or lame is he or she acceptable ? " which must be answered in the affirmative. The marriage could not take place should either respond in the negative. The couple then facing each other, with their heads touching, a small gold cross was tied with a red silken string on the forehead of each, and the symbol of the Holy Ghost pressed against them. The ceremony terminated by the partaking of wine ; after which the married couple walk hand in hand to the door of the church ; but from thence to her home the bride is once more supported by her bridesmaids. The moment they are about to cross the threshold, a sheep is sacrificed, over whose blood they step into the house.

The bride and bridegroom soon open a round dance, during which money is thrown over their heads. Until Wednesday evening the bridegroom is not allowed to dine *tête a tête* with his bride. The only guests admitted that day to the family dinner are the priest and his wife. The latter passes the night in the house; and next morning takes the tidings to the bride's mother, that her daughter has happily entered on the duties of married life.

From these onerous ceremonies Helen was happily freed, since Pancaldi Bey was most liberal and advanced in his religious views, although his family were not.

So the usual Roman Catholic service only was substituted for the more elaborate Orthodox one, much to the dissatisfaction of the relatives and friends of the young man, and the young couple took their chances in the matrimonial lottery, with bright hopes of drawing its highest prizes.

CHAPTER XXII.

HARRY LEE'S RETURN. AN OLD SCHOOL
ARMENIAN HOUSEHOLD.

HARRY LEE had reached Constantinople
three weeks after the marriage of his
cousin Helen with the young Armenian;
and the shock which the tidings gave him
was almost sufficient to unsettle his reason.
For, hoping against hope, he yet had
cherished in his secret heart the conviction
of yet winning her love by his constancy
and devotion; and he had traversed all
those long weary miles of land and sea, and
made all those sacrifices, only to find the
door locked and barred against him, and
to witness the triumph of a rival.

That rival too was not even a man of his own race; but of one which he deemed inferior in all respects, especially as regarded honour and genuine manhood; and the pang was rendered the more bitter by that reflection, and the fear that his cousin had staked her future happiness on a most uncertain venture.

For although he had never resided in the East, nor even travelled there, yet, like most Americans of his class in the South, he had been a great reader, and had a very clear conception of the chief varieties of the human species populating Turkey, and their real nature and character.

The almost universal verdict of travellers and residents there had stamped upon the Armenian the characteristics of a long oppressed and long subject race, taught from earliest childhood to meet and baffle force by fraud, and oppression by cunning.

Intellectually superior to their Turkish
master, but morally if not his inferior,
certainly not his superior, preserving
their nationality as stubbornly and as
wonderfully as the Israelites, like them
dispersed over the whole surface of the
earth, without a country of their own, the
Armenians, numbering perhaps 2,000,000,
seemed as indestructible as the whilom
" Chosen people of God."

Yet, the thought that his cousin
Helen had wedded one of that race,
and identified herself with them, apart
from his affection for her, wounded his
pride to the quick : and he thought
seriously of renouncing the Turkish service,
and returning to the Brazilian colony,
which he now bitterly repented ever having
left, melancholy as had been his existence
there.

" Yes," he muttered bitterly, as

he sat in his lonely room at the Grand
Hotel, "I might have known what Fate
or Fortune had in reserve for me; and
buried myself alive in Brazil, without
building up a fool's paradise, as I discovered I had done an hour after my arrival here. "I might have known I was
a man, like Job, under a curse! First
I lost my country, and with it almost
all of my kindred, filling as they do
most of them bloody graves. At the
same time I lost all of my most
cherished illusions, and my belief that
Providence would sustain the right against
superior force, and not allow the South to
share the fate of Poland, Hungary, and
other small nationalities. Next I lost a
part of my manhood, and my power of
earning my daily bread, by being made a
cripple !"—and he glanced bitterly at the
empty sleeve pinned across his chest—

" and now, head and heart are equally
smitten by this final blow, which leaves me
no hope nor desire for the future ! "

¡˙˙ As he thus communed with himself, for
the first time since his manhood, over the
bronzed face slowly trickled the first tears,
ever welling up from their deep source in
that manly breast, hitherto steeled and
invulnerable to the poisoned arrows of the
malignant fortune, which seemed bent on
robbing him of all which could render
life endurable.

He had borne much—he had suffered
much—he had sorrowed much—and had
steeled himself with a stern stoicism
against all ; still cherishing one secret
hope at the bottom of his heart, like a
well-spring in the depths of the arid
desert. And now that well-spring was
suddenly and remorselessly dried up, and
new fountains of bitterness, like wells of

Marah, gushed up in his breast, and withered all those fresh-budding hopes.

He pondered over those terrible words of the wife of Job, which have come echoing down to so many forlorn stricken and desperate hearts through the centuries, " Curse God and die ! " and his tears were dried, and a fierce resentful sense of wrong and injury thrilled through his whole mind heart and brain, that he should be singled out as a second Job, among the myriads of mankind, to bear burdens which he, in his pain, regarded as heavier than those ever borne by mortal man before. His memory conjured up images of pain and suffering only—nothing that could soothe or solace him in this hour of his greatest trial and tribulation. He recalled the terrible story of the prisoner at Venice in the middle ages, who daily saw the walls and roof of his room closing

in upon him, until they would enclose him
in a tomb, and crush out his life. To him
it seemed such was his doom : for life,
health liberty enjoyment all had finally
been condensed for him, a stricken exile,
in this last hope, now finally extinguished
in darkness and ashes. The soul which
war, exile, poverty, the loss of a limb and
long years of suffering could not subdue,
now sickened and sought for extinction,
because a foolish and frail girl, guided
by her wayward fancies, not her heart
or reason, had chosen another than
he with whom to pass through this
earthly pilgrimage. And the strong man
again bowed down his head upon his
table, and wept such tears of blood, as
only bearded men can weep once in a
life-time !

But this paroxysm over, the native manli-
ness and long habit of endurance braced

up the suffering man again, to meet and conquer his fate as best he might.

He took from his breast the portrait of his mother, which he always wore, representing a sad sweet youthful face, with eyes full of yearning love, and gentler and better feelings came over him as he gazed upon it : and the fierce despair which had taken possession of him melted away, as the glacier melts under the sunbeams.

She had died young, but he had never forgotten the lessons she had taught her boy ; lessons drawn from the Holy Book, which alone can teach man the lesson of his own insignificance, and the duty of submission to the Divine Will, which chastens most those it loves best, and whose decrees the feeble and erring mind of man may not measure or judge.

A devout Catholic, she had inculcated

her trusting faith on the boy's plastic nature; and now, in the hour of his mental agony and heart-throes, he recalled those lessons and strove to follow their teachings, with as much humility as he might, after so long a lapse of years since he had sought to revive them,—except the brief hours spent at the convent of Nostra Senhora del Homens, in Brazil.

Dropping on his knees, he prayed long and fervently for strength beyond and above his own, to sustain and support him, and drive away the promptings of an infidel despair, whose wicked whispers seemed like inspirations coming direct from the Evil One, whose intermeddling in human affairs our forefathers devoutly believed in, but whose existence even modern science and modern infidelity have reasoned and sneered away, together with the Deity; reverting to old Roman materialism, as the substitute for revealed religion.

When Harry Lee rose up, the cloud seemed to have rolled away from his heart and brain, and his manhood to have returned to him; and, although then and thenceforward his stern sad face seemed to have caught and reflected a yet sadder shade, its old resolute expression was reflected still, and no womanly weakness was visible upon it.

He had learned the lesson, that "to bear is to conquer our fate!" and his practice was according to that conviction throughout all the coming years. Never again did he give way to the weakness of that day, but submitted and suffered in silence, in seeming if not real resignation.

He determined to be Helen's brother and friend, since no closer tie could unite them now, and would remain near at hand

to ward off any evil or wrong which her
ill-assorted union might possibly bring
upon her, and which with an ominous
foreboding he seemed to feel impending
over that head still so dearly beloved.
Carefully adjusting his toilette and his
countenance, so as to present no outward
indication of the internal storm which had
wrecked his happiness and convulsed his
soul, he descended to the dining-room,
where he found the General and his staff,
and made himself the life of the party by
his graphic descriptions of the Confederate
colony at Brazil, and of the old friends he
had left there, concerning whom the
deepest interest was felt by his auditors,
exiled to another hemisphere.

A short time after he had been duly
entered into the Turkish service, as an
additional *aide* to General Prescott, who
had charge of the cavalry, Harry Lee

summoned up courage to pay a visit to his
cousin Helen, which under one pretext
or another he had postponed since his
reaching Constantinople. He chose a day
and an hour when he knew her husband
would be absent, and engaged in his
official duties at the palace; for he had
not yet sufficiently hardened himself
willingly to witness another usurping that
place by her side which he had fondly
hoped would one day have been his own.

He learned that the newly-married
couple were for the moment residing with
the husband's family at Ortakeui—the
village on the Bosphorus next to Beckishtach, and mounting on horseback before
midday, he rode out to that place by the
hilly and picturesque road which leads
from Taxim, the suburb of Pera, past the
palace and gardens of Yildiz Kiosk, down
by the other grand palace of Dolma

Bagtche at Bechishtach, along the shore of the Bosphorus, to Ortakeui.

There he easily found the old residence of the family he sought, who were the notabilities of that somewhat squalid and tumble-down village. The Pancaldi family was one of very ancient date, and of high standing among the Armenian community of Constantinople—at once one of the richest and most hard-working among the Rayah or subject Christian communities comprised in that wonderful conglomeration of races and creeds, constituting the population of Constantinople.

For many successive generations the Pancaldis had been in the service of the state, in various lucrative civil positions, connected with the administration of the finances or the revenues. While they had grown fat and sleek in the service, they had never ostentatiously given any outward

manifestations of wealth, but on the contrary, both in their habitation and mode of
life, gave indications of straitened means,
and practised the pride that apes humility.
    The large rambling wooden house, in
which they lived in patriarchal fashion—
each branch of the family appropriating a
floor or a wing—had been left unpainted
for many years, its exterior blistered and
roughened by the storms and sunshine of
many successive winters and summers, without any attempts at reparation of battered
doors and broken shutters. There was a
general air of dilapidation and decay about
the entire building, which with but little
care and decoration would have been quite
an imposing one; being very spacious, and
surrounded by a large but uncared-for
garden, in which flowers herbs vegetables and fruit-trees seemed struggling
for possession.

The grandfather of the present family had had, in his day, charge of one of the great fabrics of the Government, and had made it his debtor through advances of cash to the amount of many thousands of pounds. Wishing a settlement of his account with the Government, he applied to the Grand Vizier, giving statements and vouchers authenticating his claims on the administration. A few days later the Grand Vizier took him into the presence of the Sultan, and to his amazement and horror, presented him as one of the most loyal and devoted of his Imperial Majesty's subjects, who having a large claim for moneys advanced to the Government, humbly begged to be allowed to depose the titles thereof at the feet of his Majesty, and humbly present it as a free gift, in token of his love and reverence for the Imperial person !

Before the astounded creditor could

open his mouth, or frame a contradiction
to this statement, the Sultan most graciously accepted the offer, with his warm-
est praise of the liberal and public-spirited
donor; on whom he then and there con-
ferred the fourth order of the Medjidie,
with profuse promises of further marks of
royal regard : and before the stupefied man
could put in a disclaimer, he was hustled
out of the royal presence and the palace.
He staggered home—like a man struck by
lightning, blinded and bewildered—to die
that night of apoplexy, leaving behind
him however a portion of his wealth,
which neither Grand Vizier nor Sultan
could reach, and which his family enjoyed.

This awkward incident did not alter the
relations of the family with the Government, nor prevent the son and grandson
of the victim from partaking of public
patronage, and filling lucrative public

posts. The Pancaldi family continued
to rank among the most influential in the
Armenian society—a society keeping itself
aloof from foreigners and from Greeks,
as well as from Turks.

Dismounting from his horse at a high,
massive gate set in a high stone wall, on
the heights of Ortakeui, Harry Lee rapped
loudly with his riding-whip, and the heavy
gate swung open, pulled by a string from
within, admitting him into a grass-grown
neglected-looking courtyard, into which he
entered. Fastening his horse to a post in
which there was a ring, he ascended a
flight of rickety wooden steps which led
up to a higher court, and reached a door
apparently leading into the mansion already described. He pulled at a bell-
handle set in the side, but its wire was
evidently broken and unserviceable, for no
sound was elicited nor did any one come

at his summons. After waiting some
time he rapped loudly on the door, and it
swung open, as had the gate, pulled by
some unseen hand from within. Entering
the passage-way he encountered no one,
but hearing a sound on the steps leading to the upper story, looked up and saw
a woman's head projected over the balus-
trade, the hair of which head looked
wonderfully unkempt and unbrushed, the
form being wrapped in a kind of loose
dressing-gown of some thin eastern stuff.

From the mouth of this person there
issued words, in some language which
Harry Lee could not understand; and he
stood helplessly staring upwards, until
another head appeared over the first
one's shoulder, and demanded in French
who he was and what he wanted—
inquiries which he promptly answered.
The shuffling of slippered feet was im-

mediately heard descending the steps,
and his first challenger, who seemed a
servant, motioned to him to ascend the
stairway after her, which he accordingly
did, and was ushered into a long bare
room, furnished only with divans running
around the walls comfortably cushioned,
but with only a table in the centre
and no chairs : a thoroughly Oriental-
looking apartment. There was nothing to
indicate that he was in a Christian, not a
Turkish house ; and as he gazed around
him in bewilderment, imagining he had
possibly mistaken the house—since Helen
could not possibly have exchanged her
luxurious home in South Carolina, and her
refined habitudes, for such a home and
such a life as this—he heard a light foot-
step behind him, turned, and saw again
the lady of his love and dreams, as fresh
fair and youthful-looking as when he

had stood under the pine-trees in South
Carolina with her, as it seemed to him, so
many ages ago. She was accompanied
by two youngish ladies clad in European
costume, whom she introduced as her
husband's sisters.

With the unerring instinct of true affection he felt that this was no home for her,
and that she had made a terrible life-
mistake in allying herself with such a
household, and such uncongenial surroundings as these; for he judged of the
occupants by the dwelling, and soon found
he was not mistaken.

As is common in many Eastern families
the Pancaldis all lived together; a mother
and two daughters, in addition to the young
man already introduced, and the sisters of
the husband of Helen. With the exception
of their unveiled faces, and smattering of
French, they might easily have passed for

Turkish women. The mother spoke or
understood no European language. She
was enormously fat, and wore a loose kind
of dressing-gown, and apparently few
other garments; her hair was in plaits
down her back; and eastern slippers, without heels, of the roomiest description, on
her feet. The daughters were smaller
patterns of the mother physically—
half-opened roses as compared to the full-
blown rose—promising to be as volumi-
nous in the course of time as she. They
wore European costumes, put on in a way
to show that it was not their habitual dress,
but only occasionally adopted, and seemed
uneasy in it. They both spoke French
volubly, were very shy at first, but soon
became communicative, and asked the
young man so many questions that he had
little opportunity of conversing with his
cousin, with whom they evidently did not

intend he should have much private conversation. They came in immediately
after her, and remained until his departure.

She tripped up to him with her usual
girlish vivacity, and as he wrung her hand
in his own, there rushed upon him the
full flood-tide of old recollections, with a
bitter sense of their altered position :—

> " And o'er his face
> The tablet of unutterable thoughts was traced,
> Then faded as it came."

Helen was too full of her own selfish
happiness and new thoughts, to notice the
depth of her companion's feelings, or the
true sentiments that actuated his half-
affectionate half-pitying greeting. For
he felt within his heart of hearts that the
latter sentiment was the stronger in his
unselfish nature, and vague apprehensions
for her future happiness came like a cloud
between him and his personal regrets.

She took his hand impulsively, her face lighted up, and she exclaimed,—

" Oh, Cousin Harry ! how glad I am to see you again. What a delicious surprise. When did you arrive ? Have you seen my father ? "

Question upon question followed so rapidly, that she did not give Harry Lee time to answer them ; but he had time to see that her manner was nervous, and that she seemed unlike her former self. ;

" I spent last night with your father, and it was he who gave me your address," he finally replied.

" How did you find him looking ? "

" Very well ! but like myself, he is not getting younger, and this climate must be trying to him."

" Oh, no ! I assure you it is a splendid climate. If we only had here the improve-

ments and cleanliness of 'our own country
it would be a paradise."

"You would have to except the dogs,
and most of the population first, I should
think ; for I never saw such ruffianly-look-
ing men as one sees in Pera! I rather
like the look of those Turks far better
than those Ar———" He checked himself,
as he remembered that her husband was
an Armenian.

"Dear Harry! why did you not finish
your sentence ? You were going to say Armenian. I should not have been offended,
and," giving a glance at her sisters-in-law,
"they do not understand English well
enough to comprehend your meaning."

"It must seem very rude of me to
speak in a language they don't know; but
I can't help it. I must talk to you in
our own honest tongue. I am sure I have
done the polite to them enough, by an-

swering all their absurd questions. I wish they would get offended and take themselves off, and leave us to chat, without those four black eyes staring at us, trying to find out what wo mean. These foreigners don't understand our free, innocent American ways."

" You must come and dine with us soon, and I will make you acquainted with my husband. You will find him so different— quite like an American. Can you come next Saturday? I shall ask my father to come with you."

"I shall be only too happy," replied Harry Lee.

" Well, then it is decided. I have so much to say to you and ask you about home, that I don't know where to begin."

" You must remember that I have not been home for years. I have been living

in South America since you left, where
I found the life more bearable than in
South Carolina."

"Why did you give it up?" asked
Helen thoughtlessly; but when she saw a
flush spread over Harry Lee's swarthy face,
she repented having put the question.

"I got tired of the life—was restless,
as a man always is out of his own country.
I thought I would try my luck in the poetic
East; but it is anything but poetic in my
mind, unless discomfort and dirt constitute poetry."

"After one gets accustomed to the
country, he prefers it to the West," responded Helen.

"I never could!" said Harry, shortly.

The conversation continued in this
constrained manner for some time, until
Helen felt more at ease with her cousin,
and they chatted about home news, and

their innumerable relatives there. The hours passed so quickly, that neither of them took note of the flight of time, and when Harry Lee looked at his watch he found he had paid, without knowing it, "an Armenian visit," which is the synonym for a long call.

" Cousin Helen! I hope I have not remained too long. Fancy, it is four o'clock ! I have been here two hours ! "

" That is nothing, Cousin Harry. The people here stay longer than that ! I am sometimes so weary when Armenian ladies call. I can scarcely understand them, and they spend the whole afternoon with us. Then their ideas are so different from ours. They can't get reconciled to my independent ways—such as riding with gentlemen, even when other ladies are with us ; and if I were to go alone I should be quite tabooed."

"I suppose they would not object to your riding with your cousin?" said Harry, laughing.

"I don't know," said Helen, "but why should they?"

Harry then bade the two Miss Pancaldis adieu, and in his best French apologized for staying so long; then, taking Helen's hand in his, he held it for some time as if loth to let it go, and made plans for the future—such as sight-seeing together. "My little cousin will act as my guide, won't she?" he asked.

"Why, certainly! Cousin Harry. I know all the sights better than Murray."

He was conducted back to the gate by the same dirty servant who let him in. As he was riding away, he looked back wistfully at the house, and saw Helen standing at the window where he had left her; raising his hat, he rode slowly away.

What bitter sad thoughts oppressed him, as he returned to his hotel that day, may be imagined. If he had found his cousin Helen surrounded by Oriental luxury, or even comfort, he would have felt more reconciled ; but to see her fair young face in such a dilapidated mean-looking house, exasperated him. He cursed his fate, and said to himself, " If I had only been here I never would have let her enter such a place ; her father ought to have been more firm, and insisted on having her to live in a comfortable home near himself; not with those prim old maids. I can see she is beginning to be disgusted with her surroundings, the next thing she will feel is that she is isolated from her former associates. Surely," murmured Harry to himself, " the world is out of joint."

Harry Lee felt very sad, as he slowly wended his way back to Pera over the deserted and desolate-looking roads which led over the hills. But he breathed a secret vow, that as he now could never be the companion of his cousin's life, as he had once fondly hoped, that he would watch over her as a brother, and protect her from the sorrows and sufferings, which he apprehended might befall her from her ill-assorted union, and the surroundings which it had entailed.

Calmed and soothed by this resolve, he resolutely smothered the pangs he felt; and with a dull aching feeling at his heart set his teeth, and determined to make duty replace affection—since the latter was denied him.

General Prescott had been prevented, at the last moment, by his duties from accompanying him; but met him at the hotel on his return and, suspecting the true state of the case, displayed so much

fatherly kindness towards him as almost
to unman him, and cause a confession,
which would have given pain to both.
But like the Spartan boy, Harry Lee concealed under his cloak the fox which was
gnawing away his heart; for he had
learned in the school of adversity,. how
sublime a thing it is to suffer and be
strong.

The General did not disguise from his
nephew, the fact of his having opposed the
marriage of his daughter with the Armenian,
until he found her health giving way in consequence of her disappointment; but finding her resolutely bent on the alliance, and
hearing nothing discreditable against the
young man, had finally to give way, and
consent to comply with his daughter's
wishes and supplications—though sorely
against his own convictions.

Both men had many thoughts on the

subject, which they did not care to communicate freely to each other. But the tie between them was rendered all the stronger by their community of sentiment and feeling, in regard to the welfare of one so dearly loved by both. Time alone could prove whether those fears and forebodings would be realized. In the interval they could but watch and wait, and pray that the anticipated evil might be averted from that sunny young thoughtless head, now filled with golden dreams of happiness.

CHAPTER XXIII.

THE CLOUDS GATHER.

THE life led by Helen in her new home, in the bosom of an Armenian family, at first amused and pleased her by its novelty, and the striking contrast which it offered to all her previous habits and associations. But this novelty soon wore off, and the society of her husband, which she could only enjoy after his daily occupations at the palace were over, could not offer her sufficient compensation for the deadly dullness of the long wearisome days spent in the company of women, so unintellectual and unsympathetic as the mother and sisters of Pancaldi—women reared in and accustomed to the dull routine of Eastern life, in its Levantine variety, and filled with all the narrow prejudices it necessarily engendered. The mother was a thorough Oriental, even as to language. The daughters, with a thin lacquer of French polish externally, at heart almost as much Oriental as the mother; and their habits of life, and modes of thought and conversation, equally uncongenial to the strange bird which had perched among them. For these young Armenian Ladies "toiled not, neither did they spin," nor did they do any manner of work, nor assist in the management of the household—a task assigned to several slatternly servant-maids, coarse copies of their mistresses.

Rising late in the day, until the evening they wore the loose garments and shuffling slippers of Eastern *demi-toilette*, and lounged and sprawled over the divans in a state of semi-somnolence, with a tattered French novel in their hands, or lying beside them. Superficially educated, with a command of tongues exceptional elsewhere, the number of their ideas was by no means proportional to their facility of expressing them ; and the creation and circulation of scandalous gossip about their neighbours and so-called friends, formed the chief staple of their thoughts and conversation with each other, and with their visitors, almost all of whom were of their own sex. For the separation of the two sexes before marriage is almost as strictly enjoined among the native Christian or Rayah population as among the Mohammedans, which naturally prevents any such social life as Western women enjoy. But if in their ways of life and habits the Armenians approximate the Turkish women, none the less is there a wide gulf which separates and alienates them from each other. The religious bigotry of the Native Christians has been intensified by centuries of oppression and contumely.

They cannot imitate the contemptuous tolerance, with which the Turkish race regard the Christian Rayah, which is easy enough for the dominant race to practise, but impossible for a subject race, conscious of its intellectual superiority over its masters, to feel or practise. Hence a Chinese wall of exclusion shuts out the one race from the other.

Disdainfully designated by the Turk as " the camels of the empire," and bearing most of the heavy burdens physically and intellectually—from the hamal or porter to the subordinate officers of state—the Armenian avenges himself by despoiling his oppressor of his ill-gotten wealth, and secretly despising him, though (unlike the Greek who has a country) he has no chance of revolting against his rule, or indulging in dreams of future independence.

Much of the hoarded wealth of the empire is in Armenian hands. They are the bankers and accountants, large real estate holders, and live their own lives among their own people, independently of other Christian communities.

Suddenly thrown into such associations and such a society as this, the American girl very soon found herself in an entirely false position, and her illusions rapidly faded away, leaving her only the bleak and bare realities which surrounded her, and which daily became more insupportable. Immediately after her marriage her husband's unremitting attentions, and the novelties surrounding her, reconciled her to the uncongenial atmosphere in which she found herself; but within a few months' time even that solace was denied her; for gradually Pancaldi relapsed into his old habits and his old life, and under various pretexts spent not only his days but his nights also away from home. When he was with her the cat-like smoothness of his manner and speech was ever the same. He was even more demonstrative than before, but the quick instinct of true affection speedily detected something false and hollow under his expansiveness; and occasional flashes of impatience showed themselves, under the wife's complaints of the monotony and dreariness of the life she was leading in the old barrack of a house, in the company of his mother and sisters.

Her only comfort and pleasure, the occasional visits of her cousin, they finally attempted to cut off from her. The female

members of the family plainly intimated
to Helen, that such visits from a young
officer to a woman as young and pretty as
herself, constituted a violation of all the
proprieties; and that their friends were
gossiping very freely about it, to her
disadvantage, and that of her over-com-
plaisant husband. Hence they gave very
decided notice to Helen that such visits
should be discontinued, as even the
presence of these female spies, at such
interviews, was not sufficient to disarm
scandalous tongues; since every one knew
that the Demoiselles Pancaldi did not
understand English, the language of the
cousins. This was the last drop in the
bitter cup, which the Armenian sisters
compelled the poor girl to drink. She
revolted at it, as implying an insult to
herself as well as to her cousin. But, to
her infinite surprise and mortification, she

did not find her husband either indignant
or surprised at such a proceeding on his
sisters' part; but evidently disposed to
approve of it, and second the proposition.
He plainly declared that what might do in
America would not answer in Constantinople; and more especially in Armenian
families, or outside of the European colony.

As to himself he had no such prejudices,
having lived abroad; " but," he added, with
a genuine French shrug of the shoulders,
" *que voulez-vous, ma chère !* My sisters
mean well by their advice and their warning, and I really think you had better
profit by it ! You can give your cousin a
hint the next time he calls, and as a man
of the world he will see it as I do ! "

Without allowing the astonished and
indignant girl a word of expostulation,
he rose, blew her a kiss from his finger-
tips in his airiest style, and humming an

air from the latest opera bouffe, slipped
out of the room ; leaving Helen a prey to
reflections, the bitterness of which it would
be hard to exaggerate. For this was not
the beginning of her disillusion, although
it was the hardest blow those loving illusions had yet received directly from the
hand of the man whom she had chosen,
against the advice and earnest opposition
of her father and nearest friends, to be
the companion of her life, "bone of her
bone, flesh of her flesh, for better or for
worse, until death did them part."

A year had now elapsed since her
marriage, and she had had occasion to
correct many of her misapprehensions as to
the real character and habits of the man
whom, in her young imagination, she had
invested with all the poetic attributes of
Haroun el Raschid of the Arabian nights ;
but whom she found to be " of the earth

earthy," as weighed against the men of
her own nationality and race, and endowed
more with the qualities and the weak-
nesses of an unscrupulous woman, than
with those of the sterner sex. Disappointed in the rich dower he had anticipated with his bride, and which old
Celia's pride in the family had induced her
to hint to him during the ocean trip—disappointed also in the influence on his own
promotion, which he supposed his American connection would bring him, through
the influence of the Minister of that
country resident at Constantinople—he
had long bitterly rued his mistake, after
the first novelty had passed.

Gradually he had relaxed his devoted
attentions to his wife, and relapsed into
the irregularities of his old life, in which
gambling had held a prominent place. But
now the inuendoes of his sisters, envious

of this girl who had superseded them in their influence over their brother, had roused his jealousy; and like all men whose own standard of morality is low, suspicious of that of others, he was ready to suspect evil and impurity, where no shadow of either existed.

His wife's earnestness on the subject kindled the dull flame of those suspicions into a glow; and though he left her with a smile on his lips, there was a hell in his heart, and an awakened anger against her which boded evil.

Happily unconscious of this, and proudly defiant in her own purity, of all false interpretation or evil tongues, Helen indignant at the distrust of her sisters-in-law, and the apparent indifference of her husband, unhappily determined to brave them all, and not deprive herself of the solitary pleasure she had in life, except the occa-

sional visits of her father, whose pressing
duties and frequent absence from Constantinople rendered his society a rare
luxury.

Harry Lee naturally had no suspicion
that any possible misconstruction could be
placed on his communication with his cousin,
—and, in his stern isolation from society,
could learn nothing of Oriental ideas and
habits. And so, in despite of her warnings,
Helen persisted in seeing her cousin when-
ever he called upon her, the Demoiselles
Pancaldi, to show their disapproval not
now being present at their interviews, but
carefully notifying their brother each time
they took place ; until a sullen suppressed
fury took possession of the young Armenian's mind, irritated already by heavy
losses at the gaming-tables, and the use
of stimulants in which he now freely
indulged to drown the memory of his

debts, and of his matrimonial mistake. Still, with the habitual dissimulation which had "grown with his growth and strengthened with his strength," the unhappy man did not permit his wife to see the state of his mind and feelings; but, on the now rare occasions of his passing his evenings with her, played the part of the agreeable man of the world, if not of the devoted husband, and played it so well as to deceive her into the belief that he had only grown indifferent to her—a belief which caused her to moisten her lonely pillow many nights with bitter tears.

Such were the strained relations between the pair, so unfortunately mated, so unhappily environed, a rapidly-growing alienation between two once loving hearts, fostered unconsciously by one who would have laid down the life he prized so little to save the woman of his secret idolatry one moment's pain—when accident precipitated a catastrophe, which might have never arrived but for the intervention of that most unspiritual god, Circumstance, playing so large a part in human affairs and yet so contemptuously ignored. For much as it may wound human pride to admit the fact, the gravest issues of our lives are frequently determined by what seems chance to our finite understandings, and while the deepest-laid schemes go wrong, accident apparently as often sets them right.

CHAPTER XXIV.

THE STORM BURSTS—THE PICNIC ON THE GIANT'S MOUNTAIN.

THE Giant's mountain, which faces Therapia on the Asian side of the narrow strait connecting the Black Sea with the Bosphorus, is one of the most conspicuous landmarks in the vicinity. Tradition and fable have busied themselves with its earlier history, and the tomb upon its summit, now regarded as a holy shrine by the Moslems and jealously guarded by two of its most pious ulemas, has its real origin lost in the mists of antiquity.

The Turks, with their habitual love of appropriating Biblical traditions to all conspicuous sites, with or without any

Q 2

congruity, having heard that the great
leader of the Israelites Joshua, had gone
up to a mountain-top to pray for victory
over the enemies of his people, in defiance
of all geographical considerations, selected
this as the spot of the great general's
devotions. They have also appropriated
the grave as his place of burial. They
describe him as a giant, who was able to
sit on the summit of the mountain and
wash his feet in the gulf below; which,
considering that the altitude of the
mountain is 590 feet, would give Joshua
truly colossal proportions. The grave
itself is twenty feet long and five feet
broad, with an enclosure planted in flowers
and bushes.

Adopting the old Roman habit of
hanging up portions of their garments as
spells against illness, these imitative
people hang up small shreds of sick

people's dresses here, and have firm faith in the remedial virtues of the process.

The pious Moslem comes here also to pray, and to drink the waters of a spring which is found on the summit.

The Greeks had quite a different legend for the place, and identified it with the exploits of their favourite hero Pollux, who slew here the King of the country, who ventured to measure his strength and skill against those of the demi-god, with a fatal result.

On the slopes of the mountain there was an encampment of Turkish troops, whose white tents relieved the arid aspect of the rugged heights. They had been stationed there for drill and discipline, and to give a taste of tent life to some new recruits recently levied in Asia Minor. The detachment was commanded by Selim Pacha, and at his invitation a picnic party

had been collected from the European
society of the vicinity, among whom were
Pancaldi Bey and his wife, his sisters not
caring to join in an entertainment of the
kind, where they would meet none of
their own special friends. General Prescott
was detained at the Seraskeriat by his
duties on that day, and could not join the
party. But Harry Lee and some of his
comrades accepted the invitation, and
with military punctuality put in an appearance at the place and hour designated,
where they found a goodly company
assembled, drawn from the neighbouring
summer resorts of Therapia and Buyukdere.

Several months had elapsed since Harry
Lee had seen his cousin or her husband,
and he was shocked and pained to observe
the great change in the appearance of
both.

Helen looked more thin and haggard, her eyes unnaturally bright were encircled with dark rings, her manner feverishly restless, and her gaiety over-loud and factitious.

Pancaldi Bey bore on his face and person the marks of dissipation, and his excited speech and gesture gave evidence of some stronger stimulus than the mere influence of social intercourse and agreeable society. His former smooth, soft speech, and cat-like ways had been replaced by a kind of boisterous and noisy levity, which sat ill upon him and seemed forced and unnatural, like an ill-fitting mask carelessly worn, and not concealing the real features beneath. Selim Pacha, in giving the entertainment to his Christian friends, had provided liberally for their appetites, sharpened by the fresh air and mountain climbing ; and the buffet,

extemporized for the occasion by a skilful
caterer, was liberally supplied with the
refreshments denied the faithful.

The mimic artillery of the popping of
champagne corks kept up quite a brisk
cannonade, and Pancaldi Bey indulged
frequently and freely, until his flushed
face and slightly unsteady gait indicated
incipient intoxication ; although he still
retained perfect possession of his faculties.

There seemed however a false ring
about his demonstrative gaiety, which
excited remark, and his wife vainly
attempted to subdue it within bounds, to
his evident annoyance and half-concealed
anger. The sentiment of pity, entertained
by the better portion of the society for
the poor woman's false position and
evident unhappiness, was deepened by the
occurrences of the day, and manifest in-
compatibility of the ill-assorted pair.

Harry Lee conscious of the Armenian's jealousy towards himself, was very guarded in not forcing his attentions on his cousin; and in fact devoted himself almost exclusively to some of the other ladies of the party.

Helen saw and appreciated her cousin's delicacy, and imitated it as best she might; and so the day wore on, with genuine enjoyment on the part of the few, with simulated gaiety on that of many of the others, until the shades of evening began to fall and gave warning of departure to the guests, many of whom had to catch the evening boat at Therapia or Buyukdere, to return into town. The bugle was therefore sounded, by preconcerted arrangement, as the signal for departure; and by two's and three's the guests began to collect at the tent, where Selim Pacha, as host, dispensed his parting hospitalities. All came to the rendezvous, after brief delay, but two; for on inspecting the returning groups, it was discovered, that neither Pancaldi Bey nor his wife were among the number.

After waiting a short time to see if the truants would return, the bugle was again sounded, and some of the young men of the party, blessed with strong lungs, shouted out the names of the absentees until the surrounding rocks resounded. But all in vain, no answer was returned, nor did the missing pair come to the appointed rendezvous. The surprise of all became apprehension, and they began to take council with each other.

Harry Lee had brought with him to the picnic on the Giant's mountain an uninvited guest in the shape of a dog, which had accompanied him from South America—a kind of connecting link with his experiences in that remote land. The dog was a Spanish bloodhound of purest breed, perfectly trained, and devoted to his master; but heedless of all the rest of mankind besides.

Whatever the latent ferocity which lurked in his blood, the creature was so well-trained as to be perfectly inoffensive, and save some casual encounters with the street dogs, when accompanying his master, he led as peaceful a life as a Parisian poodle. But one had only to lcok at the latent reserves of strength in his sinewy frame and heavy jaw, as well as the slumbering spark of fire in the red eye, to be quite sure that if aroused he would prove a terrible antagonist. Obedient to his master's order he had crouched beneath a spreading tree, and lay there motionless and apparently asleep, until at a call from his master he rose, stretched out his limbs, reared his crest, and trotted to his side, looking inquiringly up into his face, as though to demand what service was required of him.

"Search!" said Harry Lee to the bloodhound, placing under the tawny muzzle the little glove he had picked up and secreted, under an impulse he had been unable to resist, to have some souvenir of the woman he had loved and lost. The dog snuffed a moment at the glove, then ran in a circle round the open space in which the picnic had taken place with his nose to the ground; then suddenly stopping short, raised his head and gave a short sharp bay. "Search!" again said Harry Lee: and the dog, with his nose to the ground, darted along the path which led up the mountain, with an unerring intuition which no reason could have given him. "They have wandered

off to look at the scenery, and got lost!"
suggested one of the ladies of the party;
"but we shall soon find them now. 1
am sure I hope so, for it is getting quite
chilly here as the night comes on!"

The chill of the atmosphere seemed to
have affected the spirits of the whole
party, for silence fell upon them all, and
an uneasy feeling of some impending
calamity appeared to move the hitherto
joyous and animated group. Suddenly,
from the heights above rose on the evening
air the deep bay of the bloodhound, followed by the sharp crack of a pistol—then
silence again!

Harry Lee, whose nerves had been
strained to their highest tension throughout the whole day, could no longer bear
the suspense, and the suspicions which
almost maddened him.

"Let us go in search of the fugitives,"

he said, with such affectation of gaiety as
he could command, and his suggestion was
immediately adopted; several of the
young men volunteering to accompany
him up the steep path, which the dog had
indicated and followed, and which led
straight up to the very crest of the
mountain.

In the meantime events had taken place,
of which they were destined only to see
the finale. Half maddened by jealousy, by
strong drink, and the long strain on his
nervous system which was ending in *mania
a potu*, the unhappy Pancaldi had half
persuaded, half dragged his wife, up the
narrow path which led to the summit of the
mountain, on which was the Giant's grave ;
and there broke forth into bitter revilings
against her conduct towards himself, and
his base suspicions of her intimacy with
her cousin, blended with wild lamentations

that they had ever met, and half re-
morseful confessions of his own misconduct
and unworthiness.

At first the unhappy woman sought to
soothe him, and disarm his suspicions ; but
his brain was in too fevered a condition long
to continue in the same mood, and he so
exasperated his wife by his base innuendoes,
that her temper rose, and she imprudently
denounced and defied him to do his worst.
With the madness of strong drink upon
him, and a brain fast giving way under
the pressure of bodily and mental disease,
the unhappy man was driven to desperation by his wife's defiance, which he mis-
interpreted as arising from a guilty passion
for a rival.

Seizing upon her, he shouted forth
hoarsely,—

"I am weary of my life, and of you.
Now I will put an end to it. Look your

last over this fair land and sea ! for to-morrow you shall never see ! "

Helen looked into his face and saw no pity there, only the desperate resolve of madness. She felt the iron grasp of the madman tighten upon her arm, as he dragged her towards the precipice, which beetles over the strait so far below. She felt powerless to resist, and closing her eyes breathed a short but fervent prayer, and resigned herself passively to her fate, which now seemed inevitable. At that critical moment, near at hand from the pass below, rose the deep bay of a hound, followed by a series of quick sharp yelps, indicating his proximity to the object of his search. The madman paused an instant at this unexpected interruption, and his grasp upon his wife's arm relaxed. She stumbled and fell down the rocky ledge, where she lay almost without sense or animation. The next moment the tawny muzzle of the bloodhound appeared through the brushwood, as raising his head from the ground, he looked eagerly around and saw his quarry. Then he stood stock still, as though satisfied what he sought was found, and that his task was over. But to the heated brain of the Armenian, it seemed that his life was in danger, and that the dog might tear him down where he stood. With a shaking hand, and an uncertain aim, he drew from his belt the pistol which was part of his uniform, and fired at the bloodhound, now within ten paces from him. The bullet struck the animal's shoulder, and ploughed a deep furrow, from which the blood spouted freely forth, though without dangerously wounding or even disabling him.

But the fierce instincts dormant in the

animal, and which had only been partially conquered by his training and subjection to man, burst forth under the pain of his wound, the sight of his own blood, and the presence of an enemy. Crouching as the tiger crouches, with every sinew stiffened into a steel cord, with eyes which literally blazed with fury, and every hair bristling on his head and body, the blood-hound with a savage growl prepared to spring upon his assailant.

The shattered nerves of the poor wretch were unequal to meeting the collision he had provoked. He turned to fly, and the half inanimate woman could hear him forcing his way through the tangled brush-wood which skirted the precipice, followed by the dog, now baying no more, but growling savagely from mingled pain and rage. After what was but a minute, but seemed hours to the terrified listener, a shriek, long loud and desperate, rung out on the still evening air, and the fall of a heavy body from the cliff could be heard, shortly followed by a howl from the dog, which sounded like a wail of human agony—then dead silence once more succeeded.

Clambering with reckless desperation up the steep mountain side, in the direction of the sounds heard from above, regardless of the pathway and pushing his way through the tangled brushwood, Harry Lee forced his way upward, in advance of his companions, who took the surer and the longer way.

When he reached the upper ledge, on the very verge of the enclosure of the Giant's grave, his anxious eye fell on a prostrate figure clad in white, lying prone on the ground ; and rushing to the spot, he knelt down beside the insensible form

of the woman he loved, heedless that the
world contained another human being,
his every thought feeling and faculty
absorbed in her alone. A moment's
examination satisfied him that she was
not dead, but in a swoon, with terror and
agony stamped on her features, frozen
into the stupor of an insensibility, which
to less discerning eyes might indeed have
seemed death. His companions toiling
after his desperate and dangerous steps,
found him there a little later, supporting
the inanimate form of his cousin, and
wildly invoking her to awaken and live, in
terms of passionate terror and anguish.

His life-secret was revealed to them,
but he recked not of it, nor of them. The
master-passion had swept away all care
for conventionalities, or for the opinion of
others.

From mingled feelings of fear and of

curiosity, his companions continued their search for the missing man, leaving Harry Lee alone with his inanimate burden. They had not far to go to learn the truth. The occasional howl of the dog led them to the spot, where at the very verge of the beetling cliff he still stood, looking down into the depths beneath, and intermittently sending forth the plaintive sounds, which had guided them to where he kept his watch.

Peering cautiously over the cliff, which sloped down to a deserted quarry, strewn with broken boulders and fragments of stone, thence by a gentle inclination giving access to the sea beneath, they saw lying huddled together, what seemed a motionless shapeless mass, which bore the semblance of a human form, but crushed almost out of recognition, dashed as it had been from the great height upon those

jagged stones : leaving the soul without a
moment's time for prayer or penitence,
before it was hurried into the presence of
the Great Creator.

CHAPTER XXV.

HOMEWARD BOUND.

A MONTH after the events which so deeply concerned General Prescott and his family had taken place on the Giant's Mountain, one of the steamers of the French Messageries line, bound for Marseilles, was about leaving the harbour of Constantinople; and the wonderful panorama of the Golden Horn and Bosphorus looked more lovely still, bathed in the warm glow of the sun just before his setting.

From the upper deck of the steamer, many eyes rested on that picture of Nature's drawing, some with admiration, some with affection, some with indifference, and some with that yearning look with which the gazer surveys a scene which his mortal eye may never wander over again.

Among the passengers were to be observed a group of three persons, who kept apart from the rest. One a stalwart old man of military bearing, with a snowy moustache, to whose arm clung the frail figure of a woman, clad in the deepest mourning; and a young man prematurely old in face, with grizzled hair, whose empty sleeve indicated the loss of an arm, but whose well-knit figure gave evidence of the strength and activity which his countenance did not promise. The elder man spoke first, more in soliloquy than as addressing his companions: "Farewell," he said, "land of enchantment, and of disenchantment! where Nature has done everything to bless and beautify, and man everything to mar and to frustrate the benign designs of Providence! Farewell!

whited sepulchre filled with dead men's bones! Evil was the inspiration which brought me here; wise the determination of my friend, General Lee, to remain with his own people."

A fit of convulsive sobbing shook the frail frame of the woman in black clinging to his arm. The tears rained down the pale face, as she bowed down her head. She drew the black crape veil closer around her head so as to conceal her features, and in a low broken tone answered her father's farewell to the city, where she had known such brief joy, and so many sorrows and trials.

"My father," she said, "we must put our trust in God, and submit to His inscrutable decrees. Sorely tried as we have been, He still has been merciful enough to spare us to each other. What other losses and afflictions can that not

compensate for ?   When we are back again
once more at the old homestead, now
restored to you, hope may revisit us once
again, and our stay here fade into the
memory of a bad dream."

Then the younger man, who had thus
far been a silent listener to the old man's
impatient utterances, and his daughter's
response, breathing the hopefulness of
youth and of Christian resignation, took
his part in the colloquy.

"My friend and second father," he
said, "we are soldiers and men.   The
courage and faith of this frail girl shame
us both, for it is our duty to encourage
and support her, whatever else may be.
Whatever we may have suffered or may
still have to suffer, we have done what
we believed to be our duty ; we have kept
our honour untarnished.   We can and will
front the world together in our old home,

although under such changed conditions. Let me replace the sons you have lost, as far as I may, and be a brother to your daughter. In our old home there is still room and a place for all of us ; and the rod which has pressed so long and heavily upon us will be, in God's mercy, made lighter, if not entirely taken away from our weary bodies and tortured souls."

Over the old man's face, still resolute and full of pride, there passed a responsive glow as the younger man spoke. The girl looked up gratefully with tear-stained eyes, while her father grasped his kinsman's hand in assent to his appeal.

Suddenly over the Bosphorus fell the lengthening shadows of evening, quickly succeeded by the veil of night. Then up rose the silvery moon, with the almost magic suddenness of the change from day to night which characterizes the Eastern clime, and through a wide wake of soft light the ship sailed away for distant shores, bearing with her three much tried hearts, in which once more the returning rays of hope and happiness began faintly to shine.

THE END.

GILBERT AND RIVINGTON, LTD., ST. JOHN'S HOUSE, CLERKENWELL ROAD.

A Catalogue of American and Foreign Books Published or Imported by MESSRS. SAMPSON LOW & CO. *can be had on application.*

St. Dunstan's House, Fetter Lane, London.
October, 1886.

A Selection from the List of Books

PUBLISHED BY

SAMPSON LOW, MARSTON, SEARLE, & RIVINGTON.

ALPHABETICAL LIST.

ABBOTT (C. C.) Poaetquissings Chronicle : Upland and Meadow. 10s. 6d.

About Some Fellows. By an ETON BOY, Author of "A Day of my Life." Cloth limp, square 16mo, 2s. 6d.

Adams (C. K.) Manual of Historical Literature. Cr. 8vo, 12s. 6d.

Alcott (Louisa M.) Joe's Boys. 5s.

——— *Lulu's Library.* 3s. 6d.

——— *Old-Fashioned Thanksgiving Day.* 3s. 6d.

——— *Proverb Stories.* 16mo, 3s. 6d.

——— *Spinning-Wheel Stories.* 16mo, 5s.

——— See also "Rose Library."

Alden (W. L.) Adventures of Jimmy Brown, written by himself. Illustrated. Small crown 8vo, cloth, 2s. 6d.

Aldrich (T. B.) Friar Jerome's Beautiful Book, &c. Very choicely printed on hand-made paper, parchment cover, 3s. 6d.

——— *Poetical Works. Édition de luxe.* 8vo, 21s.

Alford (Lady Marian) Needlework as Art. With over 100 Woodcuts, Photogravures, &c. Royal 8vo, 42s. ; large paper, 84s.

Amateur Angler's Days in Dove Dale : Three Weeks' Holiday in July and August, 1884. By E. M. Printed by Whittingham, at the Chiswick Press. Cloth gilt, 1s. 6d. ; fancy boards, 1s.

American Men of Letters. Thoreau, Irving, Webster. 2s. 6d. each.

Andersen. Fairy Tales. With over 500 Illustrations by Scandinavian Artists. 6s. per vol.

Anderson (W.) Pictorial Arts of Japan. With 80 full-page and other Plates, 16 of them in Colours. Large imp. 4to, 8l. 8s. (in four folio parts, 2l. 2s. each) ; Artist's Proofs, 12l. 12s.

A

Angler's Strange Experiences (*An*).   By Cotswold Isys.   With numerous Illustrations, 4to, 5*s*.   New Edition, 3*s*. 6*d*.

Angling.   See   Amateur,   " British   Fisheries,"   " Cutcliffe," " Halford," " Hamilton," " Martin," " Orvis," " Pennell," " Pritt," " Stevens," " Theakston," " Walton," " Wells," and " Willis-Bund."

Arnold (*Edwin*) *Birthday Book*.   4*s*. 6*d*.

Art Education.   See " Biographies of Great Artists," " Illustrated Text Books." " Mollett's Dictionary."

Artists at Home.   Photographed by J. P. Mayall, and reproduced in Facsimile.   Letterpress by F. G. Stephens.   Imp. folio, 42*s*.

Audsley (*G. A.*) *Ornamental Arts of Japan*.   90 Plates, 74 in Colours and Gold, with General and Descriptive Text.   2 vols., folio, £15 15*s*. ; in specally designed leather, 23*l*. 2*s*.

—— *The Art of Chromo-Lithography*.   Coloured   Plates and Text.   Folio, 63*s*.

Auerbach (*B.*) *Brigitta*.   (B. Tauchnitz Collection.)   2*s*.

—— *On the Heights*.   3 vols., 6*s*.

—— *Spinoza*.   2 vols., 18mo, 4*s*.

*B*ALDWIN (*J.*) *Story of Siegfried*.   6*s*.

—— *Story of Roland*.   Crown 8vo, 6*s*.

Barlow (*Alfred*) *Weaving by Hand and by Power*.   With several hundred Illustrations.   Third Edition, royal 8vo, 1*l*. 5*s*.

Barrow (*J.*) *Mountain Ascents in Cumberland and Westmore-land*.   7*s*. 6*d*.

Bassett (*F. S.*) *Legends and Superstitions of the Sea and of Sailors*.   7*s*. 6*d*.

THE BAYARD SERIES.

Edited by the late J. Hain Friswell.

Comprising Pleasure Books of Literature produced in the Choicest Style as Companionable Volumes at Home and Abroad.

" We can hardly imagine better books for boys to read or for men to ponder over."—*Times.*

Price 2*s*. 6*d*. *each Volume, complete in itself, flexible cloth extra, gilt edges, with silk Headbands and Registers.*

The Story of the Chevalier Bayard. By M. De Berville.

De Joinville's St- Louis, King of France.

The Essays of Abraham Cowley, including all his Prose Works.

Abdallah ; or, The Four Leaves. By Edouard Laboullaye.

Table-Talk and Opinions of Napoleon Buonaparte.

Vathek : An Oriental Romance. By William Beckford.

Bayard Series (continued) :—

Words of Wellington : Maxims and Opinions of the Great Duke.

Dr. Johnson's Rasselas, Prince of Abyssinia. With Notes.

Hazlitt's Round Table. With Biographical Introduction.

The Religio Medici, Hydriotaphia, and the Letter to a Friend. By Sir Thomas Browne, Knt.

Coleridge's Christabel, and other Imaginative Poems. With Preface by Algernon C. Swinburne.

Lord Chesterfield's Letters, Sentences, and Maxims. With Introduction by the Editor, and Essay on Chesterfield by M. de Ste.-Beuve, of the French Academy.

Ballad Poetry of the Affections. By Robert Buchanan.

The King and the Commons. A Selection of Cavalier and Puritan Songs. Edited by Professor Morley.

Essays in Mosaic. By Thos. Ballantyne.

My Uncle Toby ; his Story and his Friends. Edited by P. Fitzgerald.

Reflections ; or, Moral Sentences and Maxims of the Duke de la Rochefoucauld.

Socrates : Memoirs for English Readers from Xenophon's Memorabilia. By Edw. Levien.

Prince Albert's Golden Precepts.

A Case containing 12 Volumes, price 31s. 6d. ; or the Case separately, price 3s. 6d.

Behnke and Browne. Child's Voice. Small 8vo, 3s. 6d.

Beyschlag. Female Costume Figures of various Centuries. 12 designs in portfolio, imperial. 21s.

Bickersteth (Bishop E. H.) The Clergyman in his Home. Small post 8vo, 1s.

—— *Evangelical Churchmanship and Evangelical Eclecticism.* 8vo, 1s.

—— *From Year to Year : Original Poetical Pieces.* Small post 8vo, 3s. 6d. ; roan, 6s. and 5s.; calf or morocco, 10s. 6d.

—— *Hymnal Companion to the Book of Common Prayer.* May be had in various styles and bindings from 1d. to 31s. 6d. *Price List and Prospectus will be forwarded on application.*

—— *The Master's Home-Call ; or, Brief Memorials of Alice* Frances Bickersteth. 20th Thousand. 32mo, cloth gilt, 1s.

—— *The Master's Will.* A Funeral Sermon preached on the Death of Mrs. S. Gurney Buxton. Sewn, 6d. ; cloth gilt, 1s.

—— *The Reef, and other Parables.* Crown 8vo, 2s. 6d.

—— *The Shadow of the Rock.* A Selection of Religious Poetry. 18mo, cloth extra, 2s. 6d.

—— *The Shadowed Home and the Light Beyond.* New Edition, crown 8vo, cloth extra, 5s.

A 2

4 *Sampson Low, Marston, & Co.'s*

Biographies of the Great Artists (Illustrated). Crown 8vo, emblematical binding, 3s. 6d. per volume, except where the price is given.

Claude Lorrain.
Correggio, by M. E. Heaton, 2s. 6d.
Della Robbia and Cellini, 2s. 6d.
Albrecht Dürer, by R. F. Heath.
Figure Painters of Holland.
Fra Angelico, Masaccio, and Botticelli.
Fra Bartolommeo, Albertinelli, and Andrea del Sarto.
Gainsborough and Constable.
Ghiberti and Donatello, 2s. 6d.
Giotto, by Harry Quilter.
Hans Holbein, by Joseph Cundall.
Hogarth, by Austin Dobson.
Landseer, by F. G. Stevens.
Lawrence and Romney, by Lord Ronald Gower, 2s. 6d.
Leonardo da Vinci.
Little Masters of Germany, by W. B. Scott.

Mantegna and Francia.
Meissonier, by J. W. Mollett, 2s. 6d.
Michelangelo Buonarotti, by Clément.
Murillo, by Ellen E. Minor, 2s. 6d.
Overbeck, by J. B. Atkinson.
Raphael, by N. D'Anvers.
Rembrandt, by J. W. Mollett.
Reynolds, by F. S. Pulling.
Rubens, by C. W. Kett.
Tintoretto, by W. R. Osler.
Titian, by R. F. Heath.
Turner, by Cosmo Monkhouse.
Vandyck and Hals, by P. R. Head.
Velasquez, by E. Stowe.
Vernet and Delaroche, by J. Rees.
Watteau, by J. W. Mollett, 2s. 6d.
Wilkie, by J. W. Mollett.

Bird (F. J.) American Practical Dyer's Companion. 8vo, 42s

Bird (H. E.) Chess Practice. 8vo, 2s. 6d.

Black (Robert) Horse Racing in France. 14s.

Black (Wm.) Novels. See "Low's Standard Library."

Blackburn (Charles F.) Hints on Catalogue Titles and Index Entries, with a Vocabulary of Terms and Abbreviations, chiefly from Foreign Catalogues. Royal 8vo, 14s.

Blackburn (Henry) Breton Folk. With 171 Illust. by RANDOLPH CALDECOTT. Imperial 8vo, gilt edges, 21s.; plainer binding, 10s. 6d.

—— *Pyrenees.* With 100 Illustrations by GUSTAVE DORÉ, corrected to 1881. Crown 8vo, 7s. 6d. See also CALDECOTT.

Blackmore (R. D.) Lorna Doone. Édition de luxe. Crown 4to, very numerous Illustrations, cloth, gilt edges, 31s. 6d.; parchment, uncut, top gilt, 35s.; new issue, plainer, 21s.; small post 8vo, 6s.

—— *Novels.* See "Low's Standard Library."

Blaikie (William) How to get Strong and how to Stay so. Rational, Physical, Gymnastic, &c., Exercises. Illust., sm. post 8vo, 5s.

—— *Sound Bodies for our Boys and Girls.* 16mo, 2s. 6d.

Bonwick. British Colonies. Asia, 1s.; Africa, 1s.; America, 1s.; Australasia, 1s. One vol., 5s.

Bosanquet (Rev. C.) Blossoms from the King's Garden : Sermons for Children. 2nd Edition, small post 8vo, cloth extra, 6s.

—— *Jehoshaphat ; or, Sunlight and Clouds.* 1s.

Boulton (Major) North-West Rebellion in Canada. 9s.

Boussenard (L.) Crusoes of Guiana. Illustrated. 5s.

———— *Gold-seekers, a Sequel.* Illustrated. 16mo, 5s.

Bowker (R. R.) Copyright : its Law and its Literature. 15s.

Boyesen (F.) Story of Norway. 7s. 6d.

Boy's Froissart. King Arthur. Mabinogion. Percy. See LANIER.

Bradshaw (J.) New Zealand as it is. 8vo, 12s. 6d.

Brassey (Lady) Tahiti. With 31 Autotype Illustrations after Photos. by Colonel STUART-WORTLEY. Fcap. 4to, 21s.

Bright (John) Public Letters. Crown 8vo, 7s. 6d.

Brisse (Baron) Ménus (366). A *ménu*, in French and English, for every Day in the Year. Translated by Mrs. MATTHEW CLARKE. 2nd Edition. Crown 8vo, 5s.

British Fisheries Directory, 1883-84. Small 8vo, 2s. 6d.

Brittany. See BLACKBURN.

Britons in Brittany. By G. H. F. 2s. 6d.

Brown. Life and Letters of John Brown, Liberator of Kansas, and Martyr of Virginia. By F. B. SANBORN. Illustrated. 8vo, 12s. 6d.

Browne (G. Lennox) Voice Use and Stimulants. Sm. 8vo, 3s. 6d.

———— *and Behnke (Emil) Voice, Song, and Speech.* Illustrated, 3rd Edition, medium 8vo, 15s.

Bryant (W. C.) and Gay (S. H.) History of the United States. 4 vols., royal 8vo, profusely Illustrated, 60s.

Bryce (Rev. Professor) Manitoba. With Illustrations and Maps. Crown 8vo, 7s. 6d.

Bunyan's Pilgrim's Progress. With 138 original Woodcuts. Small post 8vo, cloth gilt, 2s. 6d.; gilt edges, 3s.

Burnaby (Capt.) On Horseback through Asia Minor. 2 vols., 8vo, 38s. Cheaper Edition, 1 vol., crown 8vo, 10s. 6d.

Burnaby (Mrs. F.) High Alps in Winter; or, Mountaineering in Search of Health. By Mrs. FRED BURNABY. With Portrait of the Authoress, Map, and other Illustrations. Handsome cloth, 14s.

Butler (W. F.) The Great Lone Land; an Account of the Red River Expedition, 1869-70. New Edition, cr. 8vo, cloth extra, 7s. 6d.

———— *Invasion of England, told twenty years after, by an* Old Soldier. Crown 8vo, 2s. 6d.

———— *Red Cloud; or, the Solitary Sioux.* Imperial 16mo, numerous illustrations, gilt edges, 5s.

———— *The Wild North Land; the Story of a Winter Journey* with Dogs across Northern North America. 8vo, 18s. Cr. 8vo, 7s. 6d.

CADOGAN (Lady A.) Illustrated Games of Patience. Twenty-four Diagrams in Colours, with Text. Fcap. 4to, 12s. 6d.

Caldecott (Randolph) Memoir. By HENRY BLACKBURN. With 170 (chiefly unpublished) Examples of the Artist's Work. 14s.; large paper, 21s.

California. See NORDHOFF.

Cambridge Staircase (A). By the Author of "A Day of my Life at Eton." Small crown 8vo, cloth, 2s. 6d.

Cambridge Trifles; from an Undergraduate Pen. By the Author of "A Day of my Life at Eton," &c. 16mo, cloth extra, 2s. 6d.

Campbell (Lady Colin) Book of the Running Brook: and of Still Waters. 5s.

Canadian People: Short History. Crown 8vo, 7s. 6d.

Carleton (Will) Farm Ballads, Farm Festivals, and Farm Legends. 1 vol., small post 8vo, 3s. 6d.

—— *City Ballads.* With Illustrations. 12s. 6d.

—— See also "Rose Library."

Carnegie (A.) American Four-in-Hand in Britain. Small 4to, Illustrated, 10s. 6d. Popular Edition, 1s.

—— *Round the World.* 8vo, 10s. 6d.

—— *Triumphant Democracy.* 6s.; also 1s. 6d. and 1s.

Chairman's Handbook (The). By R. F. D. PALGRAVE, Clerk of the Table of the House of Commons. 5th Edition, 2s.

Changed Cross (The), and other Religious Poems. 16mo, 2s.6d.; calf or morocco, 6s.

Charities of London. See Low's.

Chattock (R. S.) Practical Notes on Etching. 8vo, 10s. 6d.

Chess. See BIRD (H. E.).

Children's Praises. Hymns for Sunday-Schools and Services. Compiled by LOUISA H. H. TRISTRAM. 4d.

Choice Editions of Choice Books. 2s. 6d. each. Illustrated by C. W. COPE, R.A., T. CRESWICK, R.A., E. DUNCAN, BIRKET FOSTER, J. C. HORSLEY, A.R.A., G. HICKS, R. REDGRAVE, R.A., C. STONEHOUSE, F. TAYLER, G. THOMAS, H. J. TOWNSHEND, E. H WEHNERT, HARRISON WEIR, &c.

Bloomfield's Farmer's Boy.	Milton's L'Allegro.
Campbell's Pleasures of Hope.	Poetry of Nature. Harrison Weir.
Coleridge's Ancient Mariner.	Rogers' (Sam.) Pleasures of Memory.
Goldsmith's Deserted Village.	Shakespeare's Songs and Sonnets.
Goldsmith's Vicar of Wakefield.	Tennyson's May Queen.
Gray's Elegy in a Churchyard.	Elizabethan Poets.
Keat's Eve of St. Agnes.	Wordsworth's Pastoral Poems.

"Such works are a glorious beatification for a poet."—*Athenæum.*

Christ in Song. By PHILIP SCHAFF. New Ed., gilt edges, 6*s.*
Chromo-Lithography. See AUDSLEY.
Collingwood (*Harry*) *Under the Meteor Flag.* The Log of a
Midshipman. Illustrated, small post 8vo, gilt, 6*s.*; plainer, 5*s.*
—— *The Voyage of the "Aurora."* Illustrated, small post
8vo, gilt, 6*s.* ; plainer, 5*s.*
Composers. See "Great Musicians."
Cook (*Dutton*) *Book of the Play.* New Edition. 1 vol., 3*s.* 6*d.*
—— *On the Stage: Studies of Theatrical History and the*
Actor's Art. 2 vols., 8vo, cloth, 24*s.*
Cowen (*Jos., M.P.*) *Life and Speeches.* By MAJOR JONES
8vo, 14*s.*
Cozzens (*F.*) *American Yachts.* 27 Plates, 22 × 28 inches.
Proofs, 21*l.* ; Artist's Proofs, 31*l.* 10*s.*
Crown Prince of Germany : a Diary. 7*s.* 6*d.*
Cundall (*Joseph*) *Annals of the Life and Work of Shakespeare.*
With a List of Early Editions. 3*s.* 6*d.* ; large paper, 5*s.*
Cushing (*W.*) *Initials and Pseudonyms : a Dictionary of Literary*
Disguises. Large 8vo, top edge gilt, 21*s.*
Custer (*E. B.*) *Boots and Saddles. Life in Dakota with General*
Custer. Crown 8vo, 8*s.* 6*d.*
Cutcliffe (*H. C.*) *Trout Fishing in Rapid Streams.* Cr. 8vo, 3*s.* 6*d*

D'ANVERS (*N.*) *An Elementary History of Art.* Crown
8vo, 10*s.* 6*d.*
—— *Elementary History of Music.* Crown 8vo, 2*s.* 6*d.*
—— *Handbooks of Elementary Art—Architecture; Sculp-*
ture ; Old Masters ; Modern Painting. Crown 8vo, 3*s.* 6*d.* each.
Davis (*Clement*) *Modern Whist.* 4*s.*
Davis (*C. T.*) *Manufacture of Bricks, Tiles, Terra-Cotta, &c.*
Illustrated. 8vo, 25*s.*
—— *Manufacture of Leather.* With many Illustrations. 52*s.*6*d.*
—— *Manufacture of Paper.* 28*s.*
Dawidowsky (*F.*) *Glue, Gelatine, Isinglass, Cements, &c.* 8vo,
12*s.* 6*d.*
Day of My Life (*A*) ; *or, Every-Day Experiences at Eton.*
By an ETON BOY. 16mo, cloth extra, 2*s.* 6*d.*
Day's Collacon : an Encyclopædia of Prose Quotations. Im-
perial 8vo, cloth, 31*s.* 6*d.*
Decoration. Vols. II. to XI. New Series, folio, 7*s.* 6*d.* each.

Dogs in Disease : their Management and Treatment. By ASH-
MONT. Crown 8vo, 7s. 6d.

Donnelly (Ignatius) Atlantis ; or, the Antediluvian World.
7th Edition, crown 8vo, 12s. 6d.

—— *Ragnarok : The Age of Fire and Gravel.* Illustrated,
crown 8vo, 12s. 6d.

Doré (Gustave) Life and Reminiscences. By BLANCHE ROOSE-
VELT. With numerous Illustrations from the Artist's previously unpublished Drawings. Medium 8vo, 24s.

Dougall (James Dalziel) Shooting: its Appliances, Practice,
and Purpose. New Edition, revised with additions. Crown 8vo, 7s. 6d.

"The book is admirable in every way. . . . . We wish it every success "—*Globe.*
"A very complete treatise. . . . . Likely to take high rank as an authority on
shooting "—*Daily News.*

Drama. See COOK (DUTTON).

Dyeing. See BIRD (F. J.).

Dunn (J. R.) Massacres of the Mountains : Indian Wars of
the Far West. 21s.

Dupré (Giovanni). By H. S. FRIEZE. With Dialogues on Art
by AUGUSTO CONTI. 7s. 6d.

*E*DUCATIONAL List and Directory for 1886-87. 5s.

Educational Works published in Great Britain. A Classi-
fied Catalogue. Second Edition, 8vo, cloth extra, 5s.

Egypt. See " Foreign Countries."

Eight Months on the Gran Chaco of the Argentine Republic.
8vo, 8s. 6d.

Electricity. See GORDON.

Elliott (H. W.) An Arctic Province : Alaska and the Seal
Islands. Illustrated from Drawings ; also with maps. 16s.

Ellis (W.) Royal Jubilees of England. 3s. 6d.

Emerson (Dr. P. H.) and Goodall. Life and Landscape on
the Norfolk Broads. Plates 12 × 8 inches (before publication, 105s.),
126s.

Emerson (R. W.) Life. By G. W. COOKE. Crown 8vo, 8s. 6d.

English Catalogue of Books. Vol. III., 1872—1880 Royal
8vo, half-morocco, 42s. See also " Index."

English Etchings. A Periodical published Quarterly. 3s. 6d.

English Philosophers. Edited by E. B. IVAN MÜLLER, M.A.

A series intended to give a concise view of the works and lives of English thinkers. Crown 8vo volumes of 180 or 200 pp., price 3*s.* 6*d.* each.

Francis Bacon, by Thomas Fowler. | *John Stuart Mill, by Miss Helen
Hamilton, by W. H. S. Monck. | Taylor.
Hartley and James Mill, by G. S. | Shaftesbury and Hutcheson, by
Bower. | Professor Fowler.
| Adam Smith, by J. A. Farrer.

* *Not yet published.*

Etching. See CHATTOCK, and ENGLISH ETCHINGS.

Etchings (Modern) of Celebrated Paintings. 4to, 31*s.* 6*d.*

FARINI (G. A.) Through the Kalahari Desert: Fauna, Flora, and Strange Tribes. 21*s.*

Farm Ballads, Festivals, and Legends. See " Rose Library."

Fauriel (Claude) Last Days of the Consulate. Cr. 8vo, 10*s.* 6*d.*

Fawcett (Edgar) A Gentleman of Leisure. 1*s.*

Federighi. Seven Ages of Man. Lithographs from Drawings, 7 plates. 25*s.*

Feilden (H. St. C.) Some Public Schools, their Cost and Scholarships. Crown 8vo, 2*s.* 6*d.*

Fenn (G. Manville) Off to the Wilds: A Story for Boys. Profusely Illustrated. Crown 8vo, 7*s.* 6*d.* ; also 5*s.*

—— *The Silver Cañon : a Tale of the Western Plains.* Illustrated, small post 8vo, gilt, 6*s.*; plainer, 5*s.*

Fennell (Greville) Book of the Roach. New Edition, 12mo, 2*s.*

Ferns. See HEATH.

Field (H. M.) Greek Islands and Turkey after the War. 8*s.* 6*d.*

Fields (J. T.) Yesterdays with Authors. New Ed., 8vo, 10*s.* 6*d.*

Fitzgerald (Percy) Book Fancier : Romance of Book Col- lecting.

Fleming (Sandford) England and Canada : a Summer Tour. Crown 8vo, 6*s.*

Florence. See YRIARTE.

Folkard (R., Jun.) Plant Lore, Legends, and Lyrics. Illus- trated, 8vo, 16*s.*

Forbes (H. O.) Naturalist's Wanderings in the Eastern Archi· pelago. Illustrated, 8vo, 21*s*.

Foreign Countries and British Colonies. A series of Descriptive Handbooks. Crown 8vo, 3*s*. 6*a*. each.

Australia, by J. F. Vesey Fitzgerald.	Peru, by Clements R. Markham,
Austria, by D. Kay, F.R.G.S.	C B.
*Canada, by W. Fraser Rae.	Russia, by W. R. Morfill, M.A.
Denmark and Iceland, by E. C. Otté.	Spain, by Rev. Wentworth Webster.
Egypt, by S. Lane Poole, B.A.	Sweden and Norway, by F. H.
France, by Miss M. Roberts.	Woods.
Germany, by S. Baring-Gould.	*Switzerland, by W. A. P. Coolidge,
Greece, by L. Sergeant, B.A.	M.A.
*Holland, by R. L. Poole.	*Turkey-in-Asia, by J. C. McCoan,
Japan, by S. Mossman.	M.P.
*New Zealand.	West Indies, by C. H. Eden,
*Persia, by Major-Gen. Sir F. Gold-	F.R.G.S.
smid.	

* *Not ready yet.*

Fortnight in Heaven : an Unconventional Romance. 3*s*. 6*d*.

Fortunes made in Business. Vols. I., II., III. 16*s*. each.

Frampton (Mary) Journal, Letters, and Anecdotes, 1799— 1846. 8vo, 14*s*.

Franc (Maud Jeanne). The following form one Series, small post 8vo, in uniform cloth bindings, with gilt edges :—

Emily's Choice. 5*s*.	Vermont Vale. 5*s*.
Hall's Vineyard. 4*s*.	Minnie's Mission. 4*s*.
John's Wife : A Story of Life in South Australia. 4*s*.	Little Mercy. 4*s*.
	Beatrice Melton's Discipline. 4*s*.
Marian ; or, The Light of Some One's Home. 5*s*.	No Longer a Child. 4*s*.
	Golden Gifts. 4*s*.
Silken Cords and Iron Fetters. 4*s*.	Two Sides to Every Question. 4*s*.
Into the Light. 4*s*.	Master of Ralston. 4*s*.

Frank's Ranche ; or, My Holiday in the Rockies. A Contribution to the Inquiry into What we are to Do with our Boys. 5*s*.

French. See JULIEN.

Froissart. See LANIER.

Fuller (Edward) Fellow Travellers. 3*s*. 6*d*.

GALE (F. ; the Old Buffer) Modern English Sports : their Use and Abuse. Crown 8vo, 6*s*. ; a few large paper copies, 10*s*. 6*d*.

Galloway (W. B.) Chalk and Flint Formation. 2*s*. 6*d*.

Gane (D. N.) New South Wales and Victoria in 1885. 5*s.*

Geary (Grattan) Burma after the Conquest. 7*s.* 6*d.*

Gentle Life (Queen Edition). 2 vols. in 1, small 4to, 6*s.*

THE GENTLE LIFE SERIES.

Price 6*s.* each ; or in calf extra, price 10*s.* 6*d.* ; Smaller Edition, cloth extra, 2*s.* 6*d.*, except where price is named.

The Gentle Life. Essays in aid of the Formation of Character of Gentlemen and Gentlewomen.

About in the World. Essays by Author of " The Gentle Life."

Like unto Christ. A New Translation of Thomas à Kempis' " De Imitatione Christi."

Familiar Words. An Index Verborum, or Quotation Hand-book. 6*s.*

Essays by Montaigne. Edited and Annotated by the Author of "The Gentle Life."

The Gentle Life. 2nd Series.

The Silent Hour: Essays, Original and Selected. By the Author of "The Gentle Life."

Half-Length Portraits. Short Studies of Notable Persons. By J. HAIN FRISWELL.

Essays on English Writers, for the Self-improvement of Students in English Literature.

Other People's Windows. By J. HAIN FRISWELL. 6*s.*

A Man's Thoughts. By J. HAIN FRISWELL.

The Countess of Pembroke's Arcadia. By Sir PHILIP SIDNEY. New Edition, 6*s.*

George Eliot: a Critical Study of her Life. By G. W. COOKE. Crown 8vo, 10*s.* 6*d.*

Germany. By S. BARING-GOULD. Crown 8vo, 3*s.* 6*d.*

Gilder (W. H.) Ice-Pack and Tundra. An Account of the Search for the "Jeannette." 8vo, 18*s.*

—— *Schwatka's Search.* Sledging in quest of the Franklin Records. Illustrated, 8vo, 12*s.* 6*d.*

Gisborne (W.) New Zealand Rulers and Statesmen. With Portraits. Crown 8vo, 7*s.* 6*d.*

Gordon (*General*) *Private Diary in China.* Edited by S. MOSSMAN. Crown 8vo, 7s. 6d.

Gordon (*J. E. H., B.A. Cantab.*) *Four Lectures on Electric* Induction at the Royal Institution, 1878-9. Illust., square 16mo, 3s.

—— *Electric Lighting.* Illustrated, 8vo, 18s.

—— *Physical Treatise on Electricity and Magnetism.* 2nd Edition, enlarged, with coloured, full-page,&c., Illust. 2 vols., 8vo, 42s.

—— *Electricity for Schools.* Illustrated. Crown 8vo, 5s.

Gouffé (*Jules*) *Royal Cookery Book.* Translated and adapted for English use by ALPHONSE GOUFFÉ, Head Pastrycook to the Queen. New Edition, with plates in colours, Woodcuts, &c., 8vo gilt edges, 42s.

—— Domestic Edition, half-bound, 10s. 6d.

Grant (*General, U.S.*) *Personal Memoirs.* With numerous Illustrations, Maps, &c. 2 vols., 8vo, 28s.

Great Artists. See "Biographies."

Great Musicians. Edited by F. HUEFFER. A Series of Biographies, crown 8vo, 3s. each :—

Bach.	Handel.	Purcell.
*Beethoven.	Haydn.	Rossini.
*Berlioz.	*Marcello.	Schubert.
English Church Com-	Mendelssohn.	Schumann.
posers. By BARETT.	Mozart.	Richard Wagner.
*Glück.	*Palestrina.	Weber.

* In preparation.

Greenwood (*H.*) *Our Land Laws as they are.* 2s. 6d.

Grimm (*Hermann*) *Literature.* 8s. 6d.

Groves (*J. Percy*) *Charmouth Grange : a Tale of the Seven-*teenth Century. Illustrated, small post 8vo, gilt, 6s.; plainer 5s.

Guizot's History of France. Translated by ROBERT BLACK. Super-royal 8vo, very numerous Full-page and other Illustrations. In 8 vols., cloth extra, gilt, each 24s. This work is re-issued in cheaper binding, 8 vols., at 10s. 6d. each.

" It supplies a want which has long been felt, and ought to be in the hands of all students of history."—*Times.*

—————————— *Masson's School Edition.* Abridged from the Translation by Robert Black, with Chronological Index, Historical and Genealogical Tables, &c. By Professor GUSTAVE MASSON, B.A. With 24 full-page Portraits, and other Illustrations. 1 vol., 8vo, 600 pp., 10s. 6d.

Guyon (*Mde.*) *Life.* By UPHAM. 6th Edition, crown 8vo, 6s.

*H*ALFORD *(F. M.) Floating Flies, and how to Dress them.*
Coloured plates. 8vo, 15*s.* ; large paper, 30*s.*

Hall (W. W.) How to Live Long; or, 1408 *Health Maxims,*
Physical, Mental, and Moral. 2nd Edition, small post 8vo, 2*s.*

Hamilton (E.) Recollections of Fly-fishing for Salmon, Trout,
and Grayling. With their Habits, Haunts, and History. Illustrated,
small post 8vo, 6*s.* ; large paper (100 numbered copies), 10*s. 6d.*

Hands (T.) Numerical Exercises in Chemistry. Cr. 8vo, 2*s. 6d.*
and 2*s.* ; Answers separately, 6*d.*

Hardy (Thomas). See LOW'S STANDARD NOVELS.

Harland (Marian) Home Kitchen : a Collection of Practical
and Inexpensive Receipts. Crown 8vo, 5*s.*

Harley (T.) Southward Ho ! to the State of Georgia. 5*s.*

Harper's Magazine. Published Monthly. 160 pages, fully
Illustrated, 1*s.* Vols., half yearly, I.—XII. (December, 1880, to
November, 1886), super-royal 8vo, 8*s. 6d.* each.

"'Harper's Magazine' is so thickly sown with excellent illustrations that to count
them would be a work of time ; not that it is a picture magazine, for the engravings
illustrate the text after the manner seen in some of our choicest *éditions de luxe.*"—
St. James's Gazette.
"It is so pretty, so big, and so cheap. . . . An extraordinary shillingsworth—
160 large octavo pages, with over a score of articles, and more than three times as
many illustrations."- *Edinburgh Daily Review.*
"An amazing shillingsworth . . . combining choice literature of both nations."—
Nonconformist.

Harper's Young People. Vols. I.-II., profusely Illustrated with
woodcuts and 12 coloured plates. Royal 4to, extra binding, each
7*s. 6d.* ; gilt edges, 8*s.* Published Weekly, in wrapper, 1*d.* 12mo. Annual
Subscription, post free. 6*s. 6d.* ; Monthly, in wrapper, with coloured
plate, 6*d.* ; Annual Subscription, post free, 7*s. 6d.*

Harrison (Mary) Skilful Cook : a Practical Manual of Modern
Experience. Crown 8vo, 5*s.*

Hatton (Frank) North Borneo. With Biography by JOSEPH
HATTON. New Map, and Illustrations, 18*s.*

Hatton (Joseph) Journalistic London : with Engravings and
Portraits of Distinguished Writers of the Day. Fcap. 4to, 12*s. 6d.*

———— *Three Recruits, and the Girls they left behind them.*
Small post 8vo, 6*s.*
" It hurries us along in unflagging excitement."-- *Times.*

Heath (Francis George) Fern World. With Nature-printed
Coloured Plates. Crown 8vo, gilt edges, 12*s. 6d.* Cheap Edition, 6*s.*

Heldmann (Bernard) Mutiny on Board the Ship "Leander." Small post 8vo, gilt edges, numerous Illustrations, 5s.

Henty (G. A.) Winning his Spurs. Illustrations. Cr. 8vo, 5s.

———— *Cornet of Horse : A Story for Boys.* Illust., cr. 8vo, 5s.

———— *Jack Archer : Tale of the Crimea.* Illust., crown 8vo, 5s.

———— *(Richmond) Australiana : My Early Life.* 5s.

Herrick (Robert) Poetry. Preface by AUSTIN DOBSON. With numerous Illustrations by E. A. ABBEY. 4to, gilt edges, 42s.

Hicks (E. S.) Our Boys : How to Enter the Merchant Service. 5s.

Higginson (T. W.) Larger History of the United States. 14s.

Hill (Staveley, Q.C., M.P.) From Home to Home : Two Long Vacations at the Foot of the Rocky Mountains. With Wood Engravings and Photogravures. 8vo, 21s.

Hitchman. Public Life of the Earl of Beaconsfield. 3s. 6d.

Hofmann. Scenes from the Life of our Saviour. 12 mounted plates, 12 × 9 inches, 21s.

Holder (C. F.) Marvels of Animal Life. 8s. 6d.

———— *Ivory King : the Elephant and its Allies.* Illustrated. 8s. 6d.

Holmes (O. Wendell) Poetical Works. 2 vols., 18mo, exquisitely printed, and chastely bound in limp cloth, gilt tops, 10s. 6d.

———— *Last Leaf : a Holiday Volume.* 42s.

———— *Mortal Antipathy.* 8s. 6d.

Homer, Iliad I.-XII., done into English Verse. By ARTHUR S. WAY. 9s.

———— *Odyssey.* Translated by A. S. WAY. 7s. 6d.

Hore (Mrs.) To Lake Tanganyika in a Bath Chair. Portraits and maps.

Hundred Greatest Men (The). 8 portfolios, 21s. each, or 4 vols., half-morocco, gilt edges, 10 guineas. New Ed., 1 vol., royal 8vo, 21s.

Hutchinson (T.) Diary and Letters. Vol. I., 16s. ; Vol. II., 16s.

Hygiene and Public Health. Edited by A. H. BUCK, M.D. Illustrated. 2 vols., royal 8vo, 42s.

Hymnal Companion of Common Prayer. See BICKERSTETH.

ILLUSTRATED Text-Books of Art-Education. Edited by EDWARD J. POYNTER, R. A. Each Volume contains numerous Illustrations, and is strongly bound for Students, price 5s. Now ready :—

PAINTING.

Classic and Italian. By PERCY R. HEAD.
German, Flemish, and Dutch.

French and Spanish.
English and American.

ARCHITECTURE.

Classic and Early Christian.
Gothic and Renaissance. By T. ROGER SMITH.

SCULPTURE.

Antique: Egyptian and Greek.
Renaissance and Modern. By LEADER SCOTT.

Index to the English Catalogue, Jan., 1874, *to Dec.*, 1880. Royal 8vo, half-morocco, 18s.

Indian Garden Series. See ROBINSON (PHIL.).

Irving (Henry) Impressions of America. By J. HATTON. 2 vols., 21s.; New Edition, 1 vol., 6s.

Irving (Washington). Complete Library Edition of his Works in 27 Vols., Copyright, Unabridged, and with the Author's Latest Revisions, called the "Geoffrey Crayon" Edition, handsomely printed in large square 8vo, on superfine laid paper. Each volume, of about 500 pages, fully Illustrated. 12s. 6d. per vol. *See also* "Little Britain."

——————————— ("American Men of Letters.") 2s. 6d.

JAMES (C.) Curiosities of Law and Lawyers. 8vo, 7s. 6d

Japan. See ANDERSON, AUDSLEY, also MORSE.

Jerdon (Gertrude) Key-hole Country. Illustrated. Crown 8vo, cloth, 5s.

Johnston (H. H.) River Congo, from its Mouth to Bolobo. New Edition, 8vo, 21s.

Jones (Major) Heroes of Industry. Biographies with Portraits. 7s. 6d.

—————— *The Emigrants' Friend.* A Complete Guide to the United States. New Edition. 2s. 6d.

Julien (F.) English Student's French Examiner. 16mo, 2s.

——— *First Lessons in Conversational French Grammar.* Crown 8vo, 1s.

———*French at Home and at School.* Book I., Accidence, &c. Square crown 8vo, 2s.

Julien (F.) Conversational French Reader. 16mo, cloth, 2s. 6d
———— *Petites Leçons de Conversation et de Grammaire.* 3s.
———— *Phrases of Daily Use.* Limp cloth, 6d.
———— *Petites Leçons and Phrases.* 3s. 6d.

K*EMPIS (Thomas à) Daily Text-Book.* Square 16mo,
     2s. 6d.; interleaved as a Birthday Book, 3s. 6d.
Kent's Commentaries : an Abridgment for Students of American
     Law. By EDEN F. THOMPSON 10s. 6d.
Kerr (W. M.) Far Interior : Cape of Good Hope, across the
     Zambesi, to the Lake Regions. Illustrated from Sketches, 2 vols.
     8vo, 32s.
Kershaw (S. W.) Protestants from France in their English
     Home. Crown 8vo, 6s.
Kielland. Skipper Worsé. By the Earl of Ducie. Cr. 8vo, 10s.6d.
Kingston (W. H. G.) Works. Illustrated, 16mo, gilt edges,
     7s. 6d.; plainer binding, plain edges, 5s. each.

Heir of Kilfinnan.	Two Supercargoes.
Dick Cheveley.	With Axe and Rifle.
Snow-Shoes and Canoes.	

Kingsley (Rose) Children of Westminster Abbey : Studies in
     English History. 5s.
Knight (E. F.) Albania and Montenegro. Illust. 8vo, 12s. 6d.
Knight (E. J.) Cruise of the "Falcon." A Voyage to South
     America in a 30-Ton Yacht. Illust. New Ed. 2 vols., cr. 8vo, 24s.
Kunhardt. Small Yachts : Design and Construction. 35s.

L*AMB (Charles) Essays of Elia.* With over 100 designs
     by C. O. MURRAY. 6s.
Lanier's Works. Illustrated, crown 8vo, gilt edges, 7s. 6d.
     each.

Boy's King Arthur.	Boy's Percy: Ballads of Love and
Boy's Froissart.	Adventure, selected from the
Boy's Mabinogion; Original Welsh	"Reliques."
Legends of King Arthur.	

Lansdell (H.) Through Siberia. 2 vols., 8vo, 30s.; 1 vol., 10s. 6d.
———— *Russia in Central Asia.* Illustrated. 2 vols, 42s.
Larden (W.) School Course on Heat. Second Edition, Illust. 5s.

Leonardo da Vinci's Literary Works. Edited by Dr. JEAN
PAUL RICHTER. Containing his Writings on Painting, Sculpture,
and Architecture, his Philosophical Maxims, Humorous Writings, and
Miscellaneous Notes on Personal Events, on his Contemporaries, on
Literature, &c. ; published from Manuscripts. 2 vols., imperial 8vo,
containing about 200 Drawings in Autotype Reproductions, and numerous other Illustrations. Twelve Guineas.

Le Plongeon. Sacred Mysteries among the Mayas and the
Quiches. 12s. 6d.

Library of Religious Poetry. Best Poems of all Ages. Edited
by SCHAFF and GILMAN. Royal 8vo, 21s.; cheaper binding, 10s. 6d.

Lindsay (W. S.) History of Merchant Shipping. Over 150
Illustrations, Maps, and Charts. In 4 vols., demy 8vo, cloth extra.
Vols. 1 and 2, 11s. each ; vols. 3 and 4, 14s. each. 4 vols., 50s.

Little Britain, The Spectre Bridegroom, and *Legend of Sleeepy*
Hollow. By WASHINGTON IRVING. An entirely New *Édition de
luxe.* Illustrated by 120 very fine Engravings on Wood, by Mr.
J. D. COOPER. Designed by Mr. CHARLES O. MURRAY. Re-issue,
square crown 8vo, cloth, 6s.

Low's Standard Library of Travel and Adventure. Crown 8vo,
uniform in cloth extra, 7s. 6d., except where price is given.

1. The Great Lone Land. By Major W. F. BUTLER, C.B.
2. The Wild North Land. By Major W. F. BUTLER, C.B.
3. How I found Livingstone. By H. M. STANLEY.
4. Through the Dark Continent. By H. M. STANLEY. 12s. 6d.
5. The Threshold of the Unknown Region. By C. R. MARK-
   HAM. (4th Edition, with Additional Chapters, 10s. 6d.)
6. Cruise of the Challenger. By W. J. J. SPRY, R.N.
7. Burnaby's On Horseback through Asia Minor. 10s. 6d.
8. Schweinfurth's Heart of Africa. 2 vols., 15s.
9. Marshall's Through America.
10. Lansdell's Through Siberia. Illustrated and unabridged,
    10s. 6d.

Low's Standard Novels. Small post 8vo, cloth extra, 6s. each,
unless otherwise stated.

A Daughter of Heth. By W. BLACK.
In Silk Attire. By W. BLACK.
Kilmeny. A Novel. By W. BLACK.
Lady Silverdale's Sweetheart. By W. BLACK.
Sunrise. By W. BLACK.
Three Feathers. By WILLIAM BLACK.
Alice Lorraine. By R. D. BLACKMORE.
Christowell, a Dartmoor Tale. By R. D. BLACKMORE.
Clara Vaughan. By R. D. BLACKMORE.

Low's Standard Novels—continued.

Cradock Nowell. By R. D. BLACKMORE.
Cripps the Carrier. By R. D. BLACKMORE.
Erema; or, My Father's Sin. By R. D. BLACKMORE.
Lorna Doone. By R. D. BLACKMORE. 25th Edition.
Mary Anerley. By R. D. BLACKMORE.
Tommy Upmore. By R. D. BLACKMORE.
An English Squire. By Miss COLERIDGE.
Some One Else. By Mrs. B. M. CROKER.
A Story of the Dragonnades. By Rev. E. GILLIAT, M.A.
A Laodicean. By THOMAS HARDY.
Far from the Madding Crowd. By THOMAS HARDY.
Pair of Blue Eyes. By THOMAS HARDY.
Return of the Native. By THOMAS HARDY.
The Hand of Ethelberta. By THOMAS HARDY.
The Trumpet Major. By THOMAS HARDY.
Two on a Tower. By THOMAS HARDY.
Three Recruits. By JOSEPH HATTON.
A Golden Sorrow. By Mrs. CASHEL HOEY. New Edition.
Out of Court. By Mrs. CASHEL HOEY.
Don John. By JEAN INGELOW.
John Jerome. By JEAN INGELOW. 5s.
Sarah de Berenger. By JEAN INGELOW.
Adela Cathcart. By GEORGE MAC DONALD.
Guild Court. By GEORGE MAC DONALD.
Mary Marston. By GEORGE MAC DONALD.
Stephen Archer. New Ed. of "Gifts." By GEORGE MAC DONALD.
The Vicar's Daughter. By GEORGE MAC DONALD.
Weighed and Wanting. By GEORGE MAC DONALD.
Diane. By Mrs. MACQUOID.
Elinor Dryden. By Mrs. MACQUOID.
My Lady Greensleeves. By HELEN MATHERS.
Alaric Spenceley. By Mrs. J. H. RIDDELL.
Daisies and Buttercups. By Mrs. J. H. RIDDELL.
The Senior Partner. By Mrs. J. H. RIDDELL.
A Struggle for Fame. By Mrs. J. H. RIDDELL.
Jack's Courtship. By W. CLARK RUSSELL.
John Holdsworth. By W. CLARK RUSSELL.
A Sailor's Sweetheart. By W. CLARK RUSSELL.
Sea Queen. By W. CLARK RUSSELL
Watch Below. By W. CLARK RUSSELL.
Strange Voyage. By W. CLARK RUSSELL.
Wreck of the Grosvenor. By W. CLARK RUSSELL.
The Lady Maud. By W. CLARK RUSSELL.
Little Loo. By W. CLARK RUSSELL.
The Late Mrs. Null. By FRANK R. STOCKTON.
My Wife and I. By Mrs. BEECHER STOWE.
Poganuc People, their Loves and Lives. By Mrs. B. STOWE.

Low's Standard Novels—continued.

Ben Hur: a Tale of the Christ. By LEW. WALLACE.
Anne. By CONSTANCE FENIMORE WOOLSON.
East Angels. By CONSTANCE FENIMORE WOOLSON.
For the Major. By CONSTANCE FENIMORE WOOLSON. 5*s.*
French Heiress in her own Chateau.

Low's Handbook to the Charities of London. Edited and revised to date. Yearly, cloth, 1*s.* 6*d.*; paper, 1*s.*

*M*C*CORMICK (R.).* *Voyages of Discovery in the Arctic and* Antarctic Seas in the "Erebus" and "Terror," in Search of Sir John Franklin, &c. With Maps and Lithos. 2 vols., royal 8vo, 52*s.* 6*d.*

MacDonald (G.) Orts. Small post 8vo, 6*s.*

———— See also " Low's Standard Novels."

Mackay (Charles) New Glossary of Obscure Words in Shake- speare. 21*s.*

Macgregor (John) "Rob Roy" on the Baltic. 3rd Edition, small post 8vo, 2*s.* 6*d.*; cloth, gilt edges, 3*s.* 6*d.*

———— *A Thousand Miles in the "Rob Roy" Canoe.* 11th Edition, small post 8vo, 2*s.* 6*d.*; cloth, gilt edges, 3*s.* 6*d.*

———— *Voyage Alone in the Yawl " Rob Roy."* New Edition with additions, small post 8vo, 5*s.*; 3*s.* 6*d.* and 2*s.* 6*d.*

McLellan's Own Story : The War for the Union. Illustrations and maps. 18*s.*

Macquoid (Mrs.). See LOW'S STANDARD NOVELS.

Magazine. See DECORATION, ENGLISH ETCHINGS, HARPER.

Maginn (W.) Miscellanies. Prose and Verse. With Memoir. 2 vols., crown 8vo, 24*s.*

Main (Mrs.; Mrs. Fred Burnaby) High Life and Towers of Silence. Illustrated, square 8vo, 10*s.* 6*d.*

Manitoba. See BRYCE.

Manning (E. F.) Delightful Thames. Illustrated. 4to, fancy-boards, 5*s.*

Markham (C. R.) The Threshold of the Unknown Region. Crown 8vo, with Four Maps. 4th Edition. Cloth extra, 10*s.* 6*d.*

———— *War between Peru and Chili, 1879-1881.* Third Ed. Crown 8vo, with Maps, 10*s.* 6*d.*

———— See also "Foreign Countries."

Marshall (W. G.) Through America. New Ed., cr. 8vo, 7*s.* 6*d.*

Martin (*J. W.*) *Float Fishing and Spinning in the Nottingham* Style. New Edition. Crown 8vo, 2*s.* 6*d.*

Maury (*Commander*) *Physical Geography of the Sea, and its* Meteorology. New Edition, with Charts and Diagrams, cr. 8vo, 6*s.*

Men of Mark : a Gallery of Contemporary Portraits of the most Eminent Men of the Day, specially taken from Life. Complete in Seven Vols., 4to, handsomely bound, cloth, gilt edges, 25*s.* each.

Mendelssohn Family (*The*), 1729—1847. From Letters and Journals. Translated. New Edition, 2 vols., 8vo, 30*s.*

Mendelssohn. See also " Great Musicians."

Merrifield's Nautical Astronomy. Crown 8vo, 7*s.* 6*d.*

Merrylees (*J.*) *Carlsbad and its Environs.* 7*s.* 6*d.* ; roan, 9*s.*

Mitchell (*D. G. ; Ik. Marvel*) *Works.* Uniform Edition, small 8vo, 5*s.* each.

Bound together.	Reveries of a Bachelor.
Doctor Johns.	Seven Stories, Basement and Attic.
Dream Life.	Wet Days at Edgewood.
Out-of-Town Places.	

Mitford (*Mary Russell*) *Our Village.* With 12 full-page and 157 smaller Cuts. Cr. 4to, cloth, gilt edges, 21*s.*; cheaper binding, 10*s.* 6*d.*

Milford (*P.*) *Ned Stafford's Experiences in the United States.* 5*s.*

Mollett (*J. W.*) *Illustrated Dictionary of Words used in Art and* Archæology. Terms in Architecture, Arms, Bronzes, Christian Art, Colour, Costume, Decoration, Devices, Emblems, Heraldry, Lace, Personal Ornaments, Pottery, Painting, Sculpture, &c. Small 4to, 15*s.*

Money (*E.*) *The Truth about America.* 5*s.*

Morley (*H.*) *English Literature in the Reign of Victoria.* 2000th volume of the Tauchnitz Collection of Authors. 18mo, 2*s.* 6*d.*

Morse (*E. S.*) *Japanese Homes and their Surroundings.* With more than 300 Illustrations. 21*s.*

Morwood.   Our Gipsies in City, Tent, and Van. 8vo, 18*s.*

Moxley.   Barbados, West Indian Sanatorium. 3*s.* 6*d.*

Muller (*E.*) *Noble Words and Noble Deeds.* 7*s.* 6*d.* ; plainer binding, 5*s.*

Murray (*E. C. Grenville*) *Memoirs.* By his widow, COMTESSE DE KETHEL D'ARAGON.

Music. See " Great Musicians."

Mustard Leaves: Glimpses of London Society. By D.T.S. 3*s.* 6*d.*

NAPOLEON and Marie Louise: Memoirs. By Madame DURAND. 7*s.* 6*d.*

New Zealand. See BRADSHAW.

New Zealand Rulers and Statesmen. See GISBORNE.

Nicholls (J. H. Kerry) The King Country: Explorations in New Zealand. Many Illustrations and Map. New Edition, 8vo, 21*s.*

Nordhoff (C.) California, for Health, Pleasure, and Residence. New Edition, 8vo, with Maps and Illustrations, 12*s.* 6*d.*

Northbrook Gallery. Edited by LORD RONALD GOWER. 36 Permanent Photographs. Imperial 4to, 63*s.*; large paper, 105*s.*

Nott (Major) Wild Animals Photographed and Described. 35*s.*

Nursery Playmates (Prince of). 217 Coloured Pictures for · Children by eminent Artists. Folio, in coloured boards, 6*s.*

O'BRIEN (R. B.) Fifty Years of Concessions to Ireland. With a Portrait of T. Drummond. Vol. I., 16*s.*, II., 16*s.*

Orient Line Guide Book. By W. J. LOFTIE. 5*s.*

Orvis (C. F.) Fishing with the Fly. Illustrated. 8vo, 12*s.* 6*d.*

Our Little Ones in Heaven. Edited by the Rev. H. ROBBINS. With Frontispiece after Sir JOSHUA REYNOLDS. New Edition, 5*s.*

Outing: Magazine of Outdoor Sports. 1*s.* Monthly.

Owen (Douglas) Marine Insurance Notes and Clauses. New Edition, 14*s.*

PALLISER (Mrs.) A History of Lace. New Edition, with additional cuts and text. 8vo, 21*s.*

—— *The China Collector's Pocket Companion.* With upwards of 1000 Illustrations of Marks and Monograms. Small 8vo, 5*s.*

Pascoe (C. E.) London of To-Day. Illust., crown 8vo, 3*s.* 6*d.*

Payne (T. O.) Solomon's Temple and Capitol, Ark of the Flood and Tabernacle (four sections at 24*s.*), extra binding, 105*s.*

Pennell (H. Cholmondeley) Sporting Fish of Great Britain. 15*s.*; large paper, 30*s.*

Pharmacopœia of the United States of America. 8vo, 21*s.*

Philpot (*H. J.*) *Diabetes Mellitus.*   Crown 8vo, 5*s.*

———— *Diet System.*   Tables.   I.   Dyspepsia ;   II.   Gout ;
III. Diabetes ; IV. Corpulence.   In cases, 1*s.* each.

Plunkett (*Major G. T.*) *Primer of Orthographic Projection.*
Elementary Practical Solid Geometry clearly explained.   With Problems and Exercises.   Specially adapted for Science and Art Classes,
and for Students who have not the aid of a Teacher.   2*s.*

Poe (*E. A.*) *The Raven.*   Illustr. by DORÉ.   Imperial folio, 63*s.*

Poems of the Inner Life.   Chiefly from Modern Authors.
Small 8vo, 5*s.*

Polar Expeditions.   See GILDER, MARKHAM, McCORMICK.

Porter (*Noah*) *Elements of Moral Science.*   10*s.* 6*d.*

Portraits of Celebrated Race-horses of the Past and Present
Centuries, with Pedigrees and Performances.   31*s.* 6*d.* per vol.

Powell (*W.*) *Wanderings in a Wild Country ; or, Three Years*
among the Cannibals of New Britain.   Illustr., 8vo, 18*s.*; cr. 8vo, 5*s.*

Poynter (*Edward J., R.A.*).   See " Illustrated Text-books."

Pritt (*T. E.*) *North Country Flies.*   Illustrated from the
Author's Drawings.   10*s.* 6*d.*

Publishers' Circular (*The*), *and General Record of British and*
Foreign Literature.   Published on the 1st and 15th of every Month, 3*d.*

*R*EBER (*F.*) *History of Ancient Art.*   8vo, 18*s.*

Redford (*G.*) *Ancient Sculpture.*   New edition.   Crown 8vo,
10*s.* 6*d.*

Richter (*Dr. Jean Paul*) *Italian Art in the National Gallery.*
4to. Illustrated.   Cloth gilt, 2*l.* 2*s.*; half-morocco, uncut, 2*l.* 12*s.* 6*d.*

———— See also LEONARDO DA VINCI.

Riddell (*Mrs. J. H.*)   See LOW'S STANDARD NOVELS.

Robin Hood; Merry Adventures of.   Written and illustrated
by HOWARD PYLE.   Imperial 8vo, 15*s.*

Robinson (*Phil.*) *In my Indian Garden.*   Crown 8vo, limp
cloth, 3*s.* 6*d.*

Robinson (*Phil.*) *Indian Garden Series.* 1s. 6d.; boards, 1s. each.

I. Chasing a Fortune,&c.: Stories. II. Tigers at Large. III. Valley of Teetotum Trees.

—— *Noah's Ark. A Contribution to the Study of Un*natural History. Small post 8vo, 12s. 6d.

—— *Sinners and Saints : a Tour across the United States of* America, and Round them. Crown 8vo, 10s. 6d.

—— *Under the Punkah.* Crown 8vo, limp cloth, 5s.

Rockstro (*W. S.*) *History of Music.* New Edition. 8vo, 14s.

Rodrigues (*J. C.*) *The Panama Canal.* Crown 8vo, cloth extra, 5s.

"A series of remarkable articles . . . a mine of valuable data for editors and diplomatists."—*New York Nation.*

Roland : The Story of. Crown 8vo, illustrated, 6s.

Rome and the Environs. 3s.

Rose (*F.*) *Complete Practical Machinist.* New Ed., 12mo, 12s. 6d.

—— *Key to Engines and Engine Running.* 7s. 6d.

—— *Mechanical Drawing.* Illustrated, small 4to, 16s.

—— *Modern Steam Engines.* Illustrated. 31s. 6d.

Rose Library (*The*). Popular Literature of all Countries. Each volume, 1s. Many of the Volumes are Illustrated—

Little Women. By LOUISA M. ALCOTT.
Little Women Wedded. Forming a Sequel to "Little Women."
Little Women and Little Women Wedded. 1 vol., cloth gilt,3s.6d.
Little Men. By L. M. ALCOTT. Double vol., 2s.; cloth gilt, 3s. 6d.
An Old-Fashioned Girl. By LOUISA M. ALCOTT. 2s.; cloth, 3s. 6d.
Work. A Story of Experience. By L. M. ALCOTT. 3s. 6d.; 2 vols. 1s. each.
Stowe (Mrs. H. B.) The Pearl of Orr's Island.
—— The Minister's Wooing.
—— We and our Neighbours. 2s.; cloth gilt, 6s.
—— My Wife and I. 2s.; cloth gilt, 6s.
Hans Brinker; or, the Silver Skates. By Mrs. DODGE. Also 5s.

Rose Library (The)—continued.

My Study Windows. By J. R. LOWELL.

The Guardian Angel. By OLIVER WENDELL HOLMES.

My Summer in a Garden. By C. D. WARNER.

Dred. By Mrs. BEECHER STOWE. 2s.; cloth gilt, 3s. 6d.

Farm Ballads. By WILL CARLETON.

Farm Festivals. By WILL CARLETON.

Farm Legends. By WILL CARLETON.

Farm Ballads: Festivals and Legends. One vol., cloth, 3s. 6d.

The Clients of Dr. Bernagius. 3s. 6d. ; 2 parts, 1s. each.

The Undiscovered Country. By W. D. HOWELLS. 3s. 6d. and 1s.

Baby Rue. By C. M. CLAY. 3s. 6d. and 1s.

The Rose in Bloom. By L. M. ALCOTT. 2s.; cloth gilt, 3s. 6d.

Eight Cousins. By L. M. ALCOTT. 2s.; cloth gilt, 3s. 6d.

Under the Lilacs. By L. M. ALCOTT. 2s.; also 3s. 6d.

Silver Pitchers. By LOUISA M. ALCOTT. Cloth, 3s. 6d.

Jemmy's Cruise in the "Pinafore," and other Tales. By LOUISA M. ALCOTT. 2s.; cloth gilt, 3s. 6d.

Jack and Jill. By LOUISA M. ALCOTT. 2s.; Illustrated, 5s.

Hitherto. By the Author of the "Gayworthys." 2 vols., 1s. each; 1 vol., cloth gilt, 3s. 6d.

A Gentleman of Leisure. A Novel. By EDGAR FAWCETT. 1s.

The Story of Helen Troy. 1s.

Ross (Mars) and Stonehewer Cooper.' Highlands of Cantabria ; or, Three Days from England. Illustrations and Map, 8vo, 21s.

Round the Yule Log: Norwegian Folk and Fairy Tales. Translated from the Norwegian of P. CHR. ASBJÖRNSEN. With 100 Illustrations after drawings by Norwegian Artists, and an Introduction by E. W. Gosse. Impl. 16mo, cloth extra, gilt edges, 7s. 6d. and 5s.

Rousselet (Louis) Son of the Constable of France. Small post 8vo, numerous Illustrations, 5s.

—— *King of the Tigers : a Story of Central India.* Illustrated. Small post 8vo, gilt, 6s.; plainer, 5s.

—— *Drummer Boy.* Illustrated. Small post 8vo, 5s.

Rowbotham (F.) Trip to Prairie Land. The Shady Side of Emigration. 5s.

Russell (*W. Clark*) *Jack's Courtship.* 3 vols., 31*s.* 6*d.* ; 1 vol., 6*s.*

―――― *The Lady Maud.* 3 vols., 31*s.* 6*d.* ; 1 vol., 6*s.*

―――― *Sea Queen.* 3 vols., 31*s.* 6*d.* ; 1 vol., 6*s.*

―――― *Strange Voyage.* 31*s.* 6*d.*

―――― *Little Loo.* 6*s.*

―――― *My Watch Below.* 6*s.*

―――― *English Channel Ports and the Estate of the East and* West India Dock Company. Crown 8vo, 1*s.*

―――― *Sailor's Language.* Illustrated. Crown 8vo, 3*s.* 6*d.*

―――― *Wreck of the Grosvenor.* Small post 8vo, 6*s.* ; 4to, sewed, 6*d.*

―――― See also LOW'S STANDARD NOVELS.

SAINTS and their Symbols: *A Companion in the Churches* and Picture Galleries of Europe. Illustrated. Royal 16mo, 3*s.* 6*d.*

Salisbury (*Lord*) *Life and Speeches.* By F. S. PULLING, M.A. With Photogravure Portrait of Lord Salisbury. 2 vols., cr. 8vo, 21*s.*

Sandilands (*J. P.*) *How to Develop Vocal Power.* 1*s.*

Saunders (*A.*) *Our Domestic Birds*: *Poultry in England and* New Zealand. Crown 8vo, 6*s.*

―――― *Our Horses*: *the Best Muscles controlled by the Best* Brains. 6*s.*

Scherr (*Prof. J.*) *History of English Literature.* Cr. 8vo, 8*s.* 6*d.*

Schley. Rescue of Greely. Maps and Illustrations, 8vo, 12*s.* 6*d.*

Schuyler (*Eugène*) *American Diplomacy and the Furtherance of* Commerce. 12*s.* 6*d.*

―――― *The Life of Peter the Great.* 2 vols., 8vo, 32*s.*

Schweinfurth (*Georg*) *Heart of Africa.* Three Years' Travels and Adventures in Unexplored Regions. 2 vols., crown 8vo, 15*s*.

Scott (*Leader*) *Renaissance of Art in Italy.* 4to, 31*s*. 6*d*.

—— *Sculpture, Renaissance and Modern.* 5*s*.

Senior (*W*.) *Waterside Sketches.* Imp. 32mo, 1*s*.6*d*., boards, 1*s*.

Shadbolt (*S. H*.) *Afghan Campaigns of* 1878—1880. By SYDNEY SHADBOLT. 2 vols., royal quarto, cloth extra, 3*l*.

Shakespeare. Edited by R. GRANT WHITE. 3 vols., crown 8vo, gilt top, 36*s*.; *édition de luxe*, 6 vols., 8vo, cloth extra, 63*s*.

Shakespeare. See also WHITE (R. GRANT).

Sidney (*Sir Philip*) *Arcadia.* New Edition, 6*s*.

Siegfried : The Story of. Illustrated, crown 8vo, cloth, 6*s*.

Simson (*A*.) *Wilds of Ecuador and the Putumayor River.* Crown 8vo.

Sinclair (*Mrs*.) *Indigenous Flowers of the Hawaiian Islands.* 44 Plates in Colour. Imp. folio, extra binding, gilt edges, 31*s*. 6*d*.

Sir Roger de Coverley. Re-imprinted from the "Spectator." With 125 Woodcuts and special steel Frontispiece. Small fcap. 4to, 6*s*.

Smith (*G*.) *Assyrian Explorations and Discoveries.* Illustrated by Photographs and Woodcuts. New Edition, demy 8vo, 18*s*.

—— *The Chaldean Account of Genesis.* With many Illustrations. 16*s*. New Ed. By PROFESSOR SAYCE. 8vo, 18*s*.

Smith (*J. Moyr*) *Ancient Greek Female Costume.* 112 full-page Plates and other Illustrations. Crown 8vo, 7*s*. 6*d*.

—— *Hades of Ardenne : The Caves of Han.* Crown 8vo, Illust., 5*s*.

—— *Legendary Studies, and other Sketches for Decorative Figure Panels.* 7*s*. 6*d*.

—— *Wooing of Æthra.* Illustrated. 32mo, 1*s*.

Smith (*Sydney*) *Life and Times.* By STUART J. REID. Illustrated. 8vo, 21*s*.

Smith (T. Roger) Architecture, Gothic and Renaissance. Illustrated, crown 8vo, 5s.

———————————————— *Classic and Early Christian.* 5s.

Smith (W. R.) Laws concerning Public Health. 8vo, 31s. 6d.

Spiers' French Dictionary. 29th Edition, remodelled. 2 vols., 8vo, 18s.; half bound, 21s.

Spry (W. J. J., R. N.) Cruise of H.M.S. " Challenger." With with Illustrations. 8vo, 18s. Cheap Edit., crown 8vo, 7s. 6d.

Spyri (Joh.) Heidi's Early Experiences : a Story for Children and those who love Children. Illustrated, small post 8vo, 4s. 6d.

———— *Heidi's Further Experiences.* Illust., sm. post 8vo, 4s. 6d.

Start (J. W. K.) Junior Mensuration Exercises. 8d.

Stanley (H. M.) Congo, and Founding its Free State. Illustrated, 2 vols., 8vo, 42s. ; re-issue, 2 vols. 8vo, 21s.

———— *How I Found Livingstone.* 8vo, 10s. 6d. ; cr. 8vo, 7s. 6d.

———— *Through the Dark Continent.* Crown 8vo, 12s. 6d.

Stenhouse (Mrs.) An Englishwoman in Utah. Crown 8vo, 2s. 6d.

Sterry (J. Ashby) Cucumber Chronicles. 5s.

Stevens (E. W.) Fly-Fishing in Maine Lakes. 8s. 6d.

Stewart's Year Book of New Zealand, 1886-87. 7s. 6d.

Stockton (Frank R.) The Story of Viteau. Illust. Cr. 8vo, 5s.

———— *The Late Mrs. Null.* Crown 8vo, 6s.

Stoker (Bram) Under the Sunset. Crown 8vo, 6s.

Stowe (Mrs. Beecher) Dred. Cloth, gilt edges, 3s. 6d.; boards, 2s.

———— *Little Foxes.* Cheap Ed., 1s. ; Library Edition, 4s. 6d.

———— *My Wife and I.* 6s.

———— *Old Town Folk.* 6s.; also 3s.

———— *Old Town Fireside Stories.* Cloth extra, 3s. 6d.

———— *We and our Neighbours.* 6s.

Stowe (Mrs. Beecher) Poganuc People.   6s.

———— *Chimney Corner.*   1s.; cloth, 1s. 6d.

———— See also ROSE LIBRARY.

Stuttfield (Hugh E. M.) El Maghreb : 1200 *Miles' Ride through* Marocco.   8s. 6d.

Sullivan (A. M.) Nutshell History of Ireland.   Paper boards, 6d.

Sutton (A. K.) A B C Digest of the Bankruptcy Law.   8vo, 3s. and 2s. 6d.

TAINE (H. A.) " Les Origines de la France Contemporaine." Translated by JOHN DURAND.

    I.   **The Ancient Regime.**   Demy 8vo, cloth, 16s.
    II. **The French Revolution.**   Vol. 1.   do.
    III. **Do.**   **do.**   Vol. 2.   do.
    IV. **Do.**   **do.**   Vol. 3.   do.

Talbot (Hon. E.) A Letter on Emigration.   1s.

Tauchnitz's English Editions of German Authors.   Each volume, cloth flexible, 2s. ; or sewed, 1s. 6d.   (Catalogues post free.)

Tauchnitz (B.) German Dictionary.   2s.; paper, 1s. 6d.; roan, 2s. 6d.

———— *French Dictionary.*   2s.; paper, 1s. 6d.; roan, 2s. 6d.

———— *Italian Dictionary.*   2s. ; paper, 1s. 6d. ; roan, 2s. 6d.

———— *Latin Dictionary.*   2s.; paper, 1s. 6d. ; roan, 2s. 6d.

———— *Spanish and English.*   2s. ; paper, 1s. 6d. ; roan, 2s. 6d.

———— *Spanish and French.*   2s.; paper, 1s. 6d. ; roan, 2s. 6d.

Taylor (R. L.) Chemical Analysis Tables.   1s.

Taylor (W. M.) Joseph the Prime Minister.   6s.

———— *Paul the Missionary.*   Crown 8vo, 7s. 6d.

Techno-Chemical Receipt Book.   With additions by BRANNT and WAHL.   10s. 6d.

Thausing (Prof.) Malt and the Fabrication of Beer.   8vo, 45s.

Theakston (M.) British Angling Flies.   Illustrated.   Cr. 8vo, 5s.

Thomson (Jos.) Through Masai Land.   Illust. and Maps.   21s.

Thomson (W.) Algebra for Colleges and Schools. With Answers, 5*s.* ; without, 4*s.* 6*d.* ; Answers separate, 1*s.* 6*d.*

Thoreau. American Men of Letters. Crown 8vo, 2*s.* 6*d.*

Tissandier, Photography. Edited by J. THOMSON, with Appendix by H. FOX TALBOT. Illustrated. 6*s.*

Tolhausen. Supplément du Dictionnaire Technologique. 3*s.* 6*d.*

Tristram (Rev. Canon) Pathways of Palestine. Series I., with Permanent Photographs. 2 vols.,folio, cloth, gilt edges, 31*s.* 6*d.*each.

Trollope (Anthony) Thompson Hall. 1*s.*

Tromholt (S.) Under the Rays of the Aurora Borealis. By C. SIEWERS. Photographs and Portraits. 2 vols., 8vo, 30*s.*

Tucker (W. J.) Life and Society in Eastern Europe. 15*s.*

Tupper (Martin Farquhar) My Life as an Author. 14*s.*

Turner (Edward) Studies in Russian Literature. Cr. 8vo, 8*s.* 6*d.*

UNION Jack (The). Every Boy's Paper. Edited by G. A. HENTY. Profusely Illustrated with Coloured and other Plates. Vol. I., 6*s.* Vols. II., III., IV., 7*s.* 6*d.* each.

VALLANCE (Lucy) Paul's Birthday. 3*s.* 6*d.*

Van Kampen (S. R.) Nicholas Godfried Van Kampen : a Biographical Sketch By SAMUEL R. VAN CAMPEN. 14*s.*

Vasili (Count) Berlin Society. Translated. Cr. 8vo, 6*s.*

—— *World of London (La Société de Londres).* Cr. 8vo, 6*s.*

Victoria (Queen) Life of. By GRACE GREENWOOD. Illust. 6*s.*

Vincent (Mrs. Howard) Forty Thousand Miles over Land and Water. With Illustrations. New Edti., 3*s.* 6*d.*

Viollet-le-Duc (E.) Lectures on Architecture. Translated by BENJAMIN BUCKNALL, Architect. With 33 Steel Plates and 200 Wood Engravings. Super-royal 8vo, leather back, gilt top, 2 vols., 3*l.* 3*s.*

BOOKS BY JULES VERNE.

LARGE CROWN 8VO.	Containing 350 to 600 pp. and from 50 to 100 full-page illustrations.		Containing the whole of the text with some illustrations.	
WORKS.	In very handsome cloth binding, gilt edges.	In plainer binding, plain edges.	In cloth binding, gilt edges, smaller type.	Coloured boards.
	s. d.	*s. d.*	*s. d.*	
20,000 Leagues under the Sea. Parts I. and II.	10 6	5 0	3 6	2 vols., 1s. each.
Hector Servadac	10 6	5 0	3 6	2 vols., 1s. each.
The Fur Country	10 6	5 0	3 6	2 vols., 1s. each.
The Earth to the Moon and a Trip round it	10 6	5 0	{ 2 vols., 2s. ea. }	2 vols., 1s. each.
Michael Strogoff	10 6	5 0	3 6	2 vols., 1s. each.
Dick Sands, the Boy Captain	10 6	5 0	3 6	2 vols., 1s. each.
Five Weeks in a Balloon	7 6	3 6	2 0	1s. 0d.
Adventures of Three Englishmen and Three Russians	7 6	3 6	2 0	1 0
Round the World in Eighty Days	7 6	3 6	2 0	1 0
A Floating City	7 6	3 6	{ 2 0	1 0
The Blockade Runners	7 6	3 6	{ 2 0	1 0
Dr. Ox's Experiment	—	—	2 0	1 0
A Winter amid the Ice	—	—	2 0	1 0
Survivors of the "Chancellor"	7 6	3 6	{ 3 6	2 vols., 1s. each
Martin Paz	7 6	3 6	{ 2 0	1s. 0d.
The Mysterious Island, 3 vols. :—	22 6	10 6	6 0	3 0
I. Dropped from the Clouds	7 6	3 6	2 0	1 0
II. Abandoned	7 6	3 6	2 0	1 0
III. Secret of the Island	7 6	3 6	2 0	1 0
The Child of the Cavern	7 6	3 6	2 0	1 0
The Begum's Fortune	7 6	3 6	2 0	1 0
The Tribulations of a Chinaman	7 6	3 6	2 0	1 0
The Steam House, 2 vols.:—				
I. Demon of Cawnpore	7 6	3 6	2 0	1 0
II. Tigers and Traitors	7 6	3 6	2 0	1 0
The Giant Raft, 2 vols.:—				
I. 800 Leagues on the Amazon	7 6	3 6	2 0	1 0
II. The Cryptogram	7 6	3 6	2 0	1 0
The Green Ray	6 0	5 0	—	1 0
Godfrey Morgan	7 6	3 6	2 0	1 0
Kéraban the Inflexible:—				
I. Captain of the "Guidara"	7 6	3 6	2 0	1 0
II. Scarpante the Spy	7 6	3 6	2 0	1 0
The Archipelago on Fire	7 6			
The Vanished Diamond	7 6			
Mathias Sandorf	10 6			
The Lottery Ticket	7 6			

CELEBRATED TRAVELS AND TRAVELLERS. 3 vols 8vo, 600 pp., 100 full-page illustrations, 12s. 6 gilt edges, 14s. each:—(1) THE EXPLORATION OF THE WORLD. (2) THE GREAT NAVIGATORS THE EIGHTEENTH CENTURY. (3) THE GREAT EXPLORERS OF THE NINETEENTH CENTURY.

WAHL (W. H.) Galvanoplastic Manipulation for the Electro-Plater. 8vo, 35*s.*

Wakefield. Aix-les-Bains: Bathing and Attractions. 2*s.* 6*d.*

Wallace (L.) Ben Hur: A Tale of the Christ. Crown 8vo, 6*s.*

Waller (Rev. C. H.) The Names on the Gates of Pearl, and other Studies. New Edition. Crown 8vo, cloth extra, 3*s.* 6*d.*

—— *A Grammar and Analytical Vocabulary of the Words in* the Greek Testament. Compiled from Brüder's Concordance. Part I. Grammar. Small post 8vo, cloth, 2*s.* 6*d.* Part II. Vocabulary, 2*s.* 6*d.*

—— *Adoption and the Covenant.* On Confirmation. 2*s.* 6*d.*

—— *Silver Sockets; and other Shadows of Redemption.* Sermons at Christ Church, Hampstead. Small post 8vo, 6*s.*

Walton (Iz.) Wallet Book, CIↃIↃLXXXV. 21*s.* ; l. p. 42*s.*

—— *(T. H.) Coal Mining.* With Illustrations. 4to, 25*s.*

Warner (C. D.) My Summer in a Garden. Boards, 1*s.* ; leatherette, 1*s.* 6*d.* ; cloth, 2*s.*

Warren (W. F.) Paradise Found; the North Pole the Cradle of the Human Race. Illustrated. Crown 8vo, 12*s.* 6*d.*

Washington Irving's Little Britain. Square crown 8vo, 6*s.*

Watson (P. B.) Marcus Aurelius Antoninus. 8vo, 15*s.*

Webster. ("American Men of Letters.") 18mo, 2*s.* 6*d.*

*Weir (Harrison) Animal Stories, Old and New, told in Pic-*tures and Prose. Coloured, &c., Illustrations. 56 pp., 4to, 5*s.*

Wells (H. P.) American Salmon Fisherman. 6*s.*

—— *Fly Rods and Fly Tackle.* Illustrated. 10*s.* 6*d.*

—— *(J. W.) Three Thousand Miles through Brazil.* Illus-trated from Original Sketches. 2 vols. 8vo, 32*s.*

*Wheatley (H. B.) and Delamotte (P. H.) Art Work in Porce-*lain. Large 8vo, 2*s.* 6*d.*

—— *Art Work in Gold and Silver. Modern.* 2*s.* 6*d.*

—— *Handbook of Decorative Art.* 10*s.* 6*d.*

Whisperings. Poems. Small post 8vo, gilt edges, 3*s.* 6*d.*

White (R. Grant) England Without and Within. Crown 8vo, 10*s.* 6*d.*

—— *Every-day English.* 10*s.* 6*d.* Words, &c.

—— *Fate of Mansfield Humphreys, the Episode of Mr.* Washington Adams in England, an Apology, &c. Crown 8vo, 6*s.*

—— *Studies in Shakespeare.* 10*s.* 6*d.*

—— *Words and their Uses.* New Edit., crown 8vo, 5*s.*

Whittier (J. G.) The King's Missive, and later Poems. 18mo, choice parchment cover, 3*s.* 6*d.*

Whittier (J. G.) The Whittier Birthday Book. Uniform with the "Emerson Birthday Book." Square 16mo, very choice binding, 3s. 6d.

—— *Life of.* By R. A. UNDERWOOD. Cr. 8vo, cloth, 10s. 6d.

—— *St. Gregory's Guest, &c.* Recent Poems. 5s.

Williams (C. F.) Tariff Laws of the United States. 8vo, 10s. 6d.

—— *(H. W.) Diseases of the Eye.* 8vo, 21s.

Wills, A Few Hints on Proving, without Professional Assistance. By a PROBATE COURT OFFICIAL. 8th Edition, revised, with Forms of Wills, Residuary Accounts, &c. Fcap. 8vo, cloth limp, 1s.

Wills (Dr. C. J.) Persia as it is. Crown 8vo.

Willis-Bund (J.) Salmon Problems. 3s. 6d.; boards, 2s. 6d.

Wilson (Dr. Andrew) Health for the People.

Wimbledon (Viscount) Life and Times, 1628-38. By C DALTON. 2 vols., 8vo, 30s.

Winsor (Justin) Narrative and Critical History of America. 8 vols., 30s. each ; large paper, per vol., 63s.

Witthaus (R. A.) Medical Student's Chemistry. 8vo, 16s.

Woodbury, History of Wood Engraving. Illustrated. 8vo, 18s.

Woolsey. Introduction to International Law. 5th Ed., 18s.

Woolson (Constance F.) See "Low's Standard Novels."

Wright (H.) Friendship of God. Portrait, &c. Crown 8vo, 6s.

Wright (T.) Town of Cowper, Olney, &c. 6s.

Written to Order ; the Journeyings of an Irresponsible Egotist. By the Author of "A Day of my Life at Eton." Crown 8vo, 6s.

YRIARTE (Charles) Florence: its History. Translated by C. B. PITMAN. Illustrated with 500 Engravings. Large imperial 4to, extra binding, gilt edges, 63s.; or 12 Parts, 5s. each.
History ; the Medici ; the Humanists ; letters ; arts ; the Renaissance ; illustrious Florentines ; Etruscan art ; monuments ; sculpture ; painting.

London:

SAMPSON LOW, MARSTON, SEARLE, & RIVINGTON,

. ST. DUNSTAN'S HOUSE, FETTER LANE, E.C.

www.ingramcontent.com/pod-product-compliance
Lightning Source LLC
Chambersburg PA
CBHW030617030726
47497CB00006B/1533